Gillian Slovo was born in Johannesburg, South Africa, in 1952. She came to England in 1964 and has spent several years working as a journalist in radical research organisations. She currently works in a film workshop and is writing her next crime novel. She lives in Dalston, East London.

Gillian Slovo

Morbid Symptoms

Pluto  **Press**

London and Sydney

First published in 1984 by Pluto Press Limited,
The Works, 105a Torriano Avenue, London NW5 2RX
and Pluto Press Australia Limited, PO Box 199,
Leichhardt, New South Wales 2040, Australia.

Text designed by Claudine Meissner
Cover designed by Clive Challis Gr.R.
Set by Grassroots, London NW6
Printed in Great Britain by St Edmundsbury Press,
Bury St Edmunds, Suffolk

British Library Cataloguing in Publication Data

Slovo, Gillian
 Morbid symptons. — — (Crime and Conspiracy)
 I. Title   II. Series
 823'.914 [F]   PR6069.L

ISBN 0-86104-773-7
ISBN 0-86104-745-1 Pbk

The process of writing this book taught me a lot. It showed me both how enjoyable it is to write fiction − and what hard work it is. But more than that, it proved to me how important are other people's ideas, criticisms, encouragement and plain help. I would especially like to thank Anny Brackx, Elana Dallas, Luise Eichenbaum, Susie Orbach and Jud Stone for meeting with me and discussing Kate Baeier as if she were real. Thanks to Gwen Metcalf for putting me up when I needed quiet and to Jeanette Lavender for her quick and efficient typing. Joseph Schwartz and Saul Fenster sat with me and plotted, and made me think that we could all do it. Ronald Segal rescued me from an all-time low, put my plot back onto paper and taught me more about writing than I thought I needed to learn. And, finally, thanks to Andy Metcalf who must be able to recite the book by heart and who gave his love and support throughout.

To Ruth and Joe

1.

The room was a mess. Any casual observer could see that. The thing was I'd been cleaning it for two hours and still hadn't got anywhere. All that had happened was that my desk had been transformed from one kind of chaos to another. Two hours earlier, it had been covered with a scattered array of papers; now the papers were piled semi-neatly into subject areas. The number of piles was daunting: made up by bits of work left over from previous projects, miscellaneous pieces of eccentric information, and leads for possible articles. The range of topics still managed to astonish me: labour relations in OPEC, a new series of tropical legumes to solve the Third World hunger problems, an unfinished UN report on how bad it was in Namibia but how nothing could be done about it (by the UN at least) and several one-page files containing possible leads (which meant that if I worked myself into a hole, I could write something that could be sold but that I wouldn't want to read myself). It was sick, sick, sick. Anyone who thinks that freelance journalism is glamorous ought to have their heads examined. 'Jangled Jewish Journalist Jams Editor's Jugular' I wrote on a scrap of paper before I threw it, too, into the bin.

Things didn't improve when I decided to tidy my hair. It would have been all right if I'd restricted myself to smoothing down the unruly black layers, but I made the mistake of staring at the mirror. Dissatisfaction stared back. My skin, I saw, was in between seasons: not quite the pallid gray it would become in the depths of an English winter, it hadn't yet seen enough sun to move into its shiny brown phase. I worried about the worry lines that were establishing themselves on my forehead and breathed an uneasy sigh of relief that bushy eyebrows were now in fashion. Then, deciding that it was all as hopeless as the room, I left.

By the time I arrived at the Carelton Buildings, my mood had only slightly improved. At least I've had a completion experience with this one, I thought to myself, as I pushed the heavy glass doors open wide enough to take me and my vast pile of books. A figure blocked my way. I moved to get round it, but it moved to block me. I glanced up.

'You're a policeman.'

He twitched his lips.

'Hey, sir,' he called, 'got another bright one here. Recognised my uniform straight off.'

His sarcasm brought a second man towards me. This one was dressed in policeman casual circa 1968 − bleached jeans, flared, with a concealed crease and topped by an off-white polo neck. Rust-brown sidewhiskers jutted from his aggressive-looking face and did nothing to hide his receding hairline. He gave me a long hard look, not bothering to conceal the way his eyes moved from my shoes to my head, lingering on the way.

'Name?' he demanded.

'Why?' I said.

'I'm on official police business. What's your name? And what's your purpose in this building?'

'What's yours?' I asked.

I admit that I wasn't contributing the more interesting part of the dialogue, but I needed to think. During its lifetime, the place had seen some eccentric goings-on, but a posse of police questioning everybody in sight was a new one on me. Nothing entered my head except for a sudden unease as the two men moved to either side of me. I was relieved when I saw Bob, the building's caretaker, climbing slowly down the stairs. Never in the best of health, Bob looked like he needed a blood transfusion. His face was the colour of dough, and his shoulders were hunched into his thin chest.

'Hello, Kate,' he said dully. 'Have you heard what happened? You'd better answer their questions. They're only doing their job.'

'What happened?' I asked.

The imitation hippy decided to go for the smooth approach.

'Okay, calm down. We're only after routine information ... from you,' and he threw a glance full of meaning in Bob's direction. 'We know your name's Kate and all we need to know is your surname and what you're doing here and then we can leave you and make both our days brighter.'

'It's Baeier,' I said, 'And I'm returning some papers to AER.'

This time I got a rough hand on my elbow. 'Don't get funny. We eat your type for breakfast. What are you doing here?'

'I'm not interested in your eating habits and I've already told you. I'm returning some books and an article I wrote to AER – African Economic Reports. Now what's going on?'

'We're investigating a suspicious death. Come this way.'

I was propelled across the hall towards the small cubby hole that serves as an administrative centre for the building. Bob interrupted by progress.

'Tim's dead. He fell down the lift shaft,' he said.

The plainclothes man let go of my hand and whirled round at Bob.

'Go up and rest, pops,' he said, 'It's been a tough day for an old timer.'

Bob stiffened and then turned away resignedly.

I was steered into a chair and found myself facing a third policeman, dressed in a light-blue suit and looking as though he would burst out of it any minute in a spasm of disgust. Images of Tim Nicholson, his face set in its habitual boyish grin, his blond hair swept untidily across his forehead, kept crowding in on me. He had been everybody's friend, a good-time boy who had melted into the distance at the first hint of personal difficulties. He would keep up a barrage of easy conversation to fill any silence and yet had seemed painfully gauche when left on his own. He had spread his charm wide, but I couldn't help feeling that he used it as a barrier to any real closeness. There had been something hidden about him, something that I had never been able to pinpoint, but which had left us friends without any real intimacy.

I wasn't given much time for my memories. I had to supply my name and address along with a number of details that couldn't have seemed more irrelevant. At one point I had to produce my immaculately typed article as evidence of my identity. The police didn't seem to have heard of press cards and couldn't have been less interested in mine.

It seemed like quite a while before he popped the question. Casual it was. Across the desk, the man in the light-blue draylon threw it out gently, his head down, his hand resting lightly on an empty pad.

'What is the connection between African Economic Supports and the Communists?'

I jerked forward.

'Reports,' I said.

He looked confused.

'Reports,' I repeated. 'African Economic Reports.'

That ruined his lead in, but he managed to continue.

'Ah, yes. Excuse me. African Economic Reports. And what is their connection with the Communists?'

I stared in amazement. This was turning into farce.

'What Communists?' I said, 'And what's the relevance of it? I thought Tim fell down the lift shaft.'

'Who told you that?' he snapped.

'Bob, the caretaker. In the presence of your plainclothes man. The one who's trying to blend.'

A flicker of annoyance crossed his bland face. It was rapidly followed by the voice of authority.

'The caretaker,' he intoned, 'is our business. We will consider charging him with negligence, but that is our concern. Now either answer my questions or you'll find yourself in more trouble than you can handle.'

'You have no right to ask these questions,' I said. 'Anyway, what's the relevance?'

The draylon gave a crackle of protest as he shifted his bulk towards me: for a moment an ingratiating grin touched his thin lips.

'Be sensible, Miss Bates,' he said. 'You're a journalist doing your job and I'm an officer of the law doing mine. We are investigating a suspicious death, and the organisation concerned has the Russian Embassy on its mailing lists. You never know what these Russians will do when they're disappointed in someone.'

He almost winked, but thought the better of it, so all I got was a vague flutter of an eyelash. I controlled myself with some difficulty.

'Baeier,' I said. 'The Soviet Embassy has a subscription to AER.

So does the Foreign Office, and half of Fleet Street and Scotland Yard. Why not go ask them why they do it?'

The man sighed. It wasn't an irritated sound, merely resigned. He'd given it a try but his heart wasn't in it. He got up, shuffled his papers wearily and gestured towards the door.

'That will be all, Miss Baxter,' he said, 'We have your address should we need to contact you again.'

'Baeier,' I said, and left the room.

Outside the door, I began to feel that I was having a field day with strange men of dubious profession. This one was a thinner variation of the others. His clothes looked like they'd been bought off-the-peg at Burtons and then mangled in a wringer immediately afterwards. His tie was badly askew, its large knot almost completely undone. His shoes were pointed without being fashionable, his shirt rumpled without being dirty. He had the look of a man who fancied himself as a great seducer and could never quite understand why he didn't make it.

'I'm a journalist,' he said.

'So I guessed. What paper?'

'The *Telegraph*. I'd like some background information. Be a dear … nice to the press and all that,' he flashed me a sickly smile.

'I'm a journalist myself. And why ask me? I'm only visiting. Surely you can find a better source.'

He moved nearer, as if trying to break the mental barrier between us. Close up, his face took on a threatening leer — and I didn't like the way his right knee was coming into play. It was more than I could stand. Without a word, I turned and walked away. Behind me his voice echoed in the desolate hall.

'Can't win 'em all,' he said, turning to the uniformed cop at the door.

'Don't even try with that one. She's a man-hater,' followed me up the stairs.

My progress to the fourth floor was marked by a sort of fluttering. Several times an office door opened, a face stared out nervously and then, seeing me, retreated relieved. Odd hushed groups of people, congregated on the stairwells, muttered as I passed. I nodded to the few people I recognised and made it upstairs.

There I saw the lift, its doors agape, its front surrounded by a makeshift barrier. Beside it a bored policeman stood in a kind of suspended animation. He ignored me, so I walked into the office of African Economic Reports.

They were all in the room. All, that is, except Tim. A heavy silence hung like an unanswered plea in the air. Ron Critchley, his mousy-brown hair standing up in knots, his National Health glasses balanced even more precariously than usual, tried a greeting that got stuck halfway. Michael Parsons stared directly at me, but I couldn't tell whether his water-blue eyes recognised more than a brief interruption to his silent vigil. His black hair contrasting dramatically with his white skin, he was handsome enough; but that day it was as though his flesh had sunk, and his fine cheekbones only made him look gaunt. Aldwyn Potter, his stolid frame oulined against the dirty windows, seemed frozen in a public school pose, hands gripped tightly behind him, head held upright. Only the slightly green tinge on his face, accentuated by his straight red hair, belied the overall impression that he was a guest at a very boring cocktail party. I sat down in the corner.

'How did it happen ?' I asked.

I got two sighs and a shrug. It was a long time before anybody found any words. Ron broke the silence.

'We assume he fell,' he said. 'Maybe he'd been drinking. He'd been hitting the bottle heavily recently. Bob found him lying ... lying there this morning.'

'But how? Surely it was impossible?,' I said.

Aldwyn found in me a focus for his tension. Decisively his stubby hand parted. His body stayed where it was, his voice resonating from within.

'What does it matter,' he said. 'Let the police do their job. Who do you think you are ... a detective?'

There was more nervousness than rancour in his speech. But still I gulped.

'I suppose I just need to know. Maybe to make it all real.' My voice sounded fragile.

6

Aldwyn heard it and gave me a brisk nod of apology. For a while we sat there amongst the litter of dead phones, their handsets lying exposed on the crowded desks. Only the occasional hooting of cars outside interrupted our thoughts. I could think of no appropriate gesture, no way of breaking through to share our feelings.

We might have been there a long time if it hadn't been for the police. With brisk, almost military efficiency, they strode into the room and ordered everybody out. Reduced to the status of children, we joined the throng that was heading for the entrance hall. The police had totally taken over: we were almost pushed out of the door. Outside, my last glance back showed only Bob's anxious face peering through the doors. There was a hand on his shoulder and fear written all over his face.

My journey home was uneventful, as was the rest of my day. I went back to sorting out my papers, just for something to do. I came across a couple of letters from Tim, sent while we were writing an article together. I put them aside to read later and lost interest in the clear-up. Instead, I picked up my alto from its stand in the corner of the room, and went to work on exercises. I was going through one of those difficult periods in my playing career: bored with the old stuff, but without the skills to move forward. Still, I was sticking at it, practising my arpeggios and waiting for the next breakthrough.

I was involved in a complex circle of minor scales when I felt a hand on my shoulder. I jumped, hitting my face with the mouthpiece, and span round to face a sheepish-looking Sam.

'I forgot,' he said. 'Sorry. It's just that I did call your name but you didn't react. Why is it you get so scared when you're surprised?'

'Put it down to early childhood experiences,' I said, as I put the saxophone down. 'Did you hear about Tim?'

Sam nodded and grimaced. With his mottled green, almost gray eyes, he searched my face to see how I felt about the news. He settled on giving me a hug, closely followed by a stiff drink.

Sam and I had originally been matchmade by some shared friends and had spent a pleasant enough evening flirting over a laden dinner table. Nothing else might have happened if we hadn't bumped into each other at one of those CSE conferences where half the people are there to catch up on a year's theory and the other half to recuperate from a year's monogamy. I'd been trying to escape from an over-zealous and badly informed acquaintance, who was giving me a lecture on the mistakes of the Portuguese left. Sam had been so busy choosing between two workshops on widely differing subjects that he'd missed them both. Indecision seemed an underlying theme in Sam's life. A mathematician on the point of getting his PhD he'd got side-tracked down an alley of algebraic topology and couldn't figure out what to do about it. His solution had been − still was − to spend more time in writing poetry than in finishing his thesis.

That weekend, we'd solved both our problems by taking off for a walk on the moors. Six months later I'd managed to convince him that I wasn't a fresh-air fiend and that I felt safer in cities, but despite this it looked like we might still be together for a while. It hadn't all been easy, partly because of Sam's four-year old, who acted like a guard dog snapping around Sam's heels. It had been hard work for all three of us, but I'd recently noticed a discernible improvement, as Matthew has taken to biting Sam's feet and throwing me an occasional smile.

Matthew spent weekdays with his mother, so Sam and I were alone. We'd planned to go out to the movies, but I no longer felt like it. Instead we went into the kitchen and cooked a not very memorable meal together. After that, I picked up a detective novel, whose plot was so obvious that I was convinced I'd read it before. Two hours later I realised that I hadn't read the book, even though I had guessed, on page six, who was guilty. Sam was sitting upright, his glazed look in complete contradiction to his alert stance. The evening had been curiously solemn: one of the first in which we had spent time without conversation. I was at the point of wondering whether here began the domestication of our relationship when the phone rang. It was Michael.

'Kate, something's come up. Could you be at the office tomorrow?'

'Sure,' I said. 'Will the police have left?'

'Oh, they've done their work all right,' he muttered. And before I could ask what he meant, I found myself holding the dialling tone to my ear.

I gave up, tired from the strain of the day and its dull aftermath. I took a bath and was asleep before I even knew that I was lying on my bed.

2.

I woke to a typical July morning: gray, wet and dismal. Sam was still sleeping, so I dressed quietly and went into the kitchen. By the look of the half-completed sentences littering the table, Sam had spent part of the night working on a poem. I moved the vestiges to one side, glanced at the finished product, which was yet more proof that Sam's poetry was travelling in a place where I could not speak the language, and took in the message to meet at Anna's later. While the coffee filtered, I set my croissant to warm and scanned the newspaper. Tim's death was there in a brief report on page one. It was treated as an accident.

By nine, I was oscillating between an umbrella and a hat. I guessed intermittent drizzle and chose the hat before making my way to the 38 bus stop. There I stood awhile, toying with the idea of heading for the overground while I studied the queue.

It's a phenomenon with few variations. People gather on the pavement without much hope. In its early stages, the congregation has little focus. When the first flash of red appears from round the corner, a line tightens, the tension mounts. Several people throw fearful glances at their nearest neighbour to assess their chances of a last-minute push. The bus draws near, the line becomes a knot. The bus stops, caught a few yards away by an articulated lorry. The ambitious or young in the queue try to make a break for it. The rest of us assess the situation with experienced eyes. Four people dismount, smugly looking at the queue. Ten people try to get on, only to be stopped by the conductor, her arms akimbo. The line dissolves, the bus moves off, and for a moment conversation about the inefficiencies of London Transport, the weather (otherwise known as the long rain), and the price of butter intervenes. Some try to push margarine, but it doesn't have the same ring, and interest soon wanes.

I stood through four of these acts before I made it up the necessary step. In my frustration, I chose a number 22, and as usual, soon had cause to regret it. By 9.55 I'd been subjected to a close view of all major traffic jams in the city area and was walking down Shaftesbury Avenue to my appointment.

Amongst the exclusive wholesale dress shops with their immaculate receptionists and fine-line blinds, the office shops selling fancy equipment at fancier prices, and the endless messengers carrying film spools, their bike radios blaring, Carelton Building stands out grimy and in need of repair. The Carelton family had made a fortune by extracting cocoa beans and supplying chocolates across the Empire. The building represents a twentieth-century expression of the family's Quaker conscience, as well as a partial solution to its tax problems. It is crammed tight with organisations housed rent-free, in some sort of ecological balance among different left-wing groups, concerned liberals and alternative businesses.

Somewhere in the Carelton Foundation is a minor clerk who has slotted each organisation into the building, to create a mix that never ceases to fascinate me. Social Options, a charity that produces fancy brochures on the conditions of the poor, has oak-panelled suites with separate secretarial rooms. Next door, the Alliance Against Advanced Technology is crammed into one big room with obligatory gray windows and huge noticeboards covered in busy instructions. The Alliance's bicycles always manage to skin the knees of visiting dignatories to Social Options; and from the floors above and below you can frequently hear the two groups arguing about this, along with whose turn it is to clean the sink.

Many other groups have settled the building, sharing offices, desks or floor space. When I arrived at AER's office, it looked as though a representative from each of them was gathered there. Clothes ranged from the standard scruffy, unchanged with the years, through a minority interest in modern fashion, to the smart casual of the up-and-coming alternative business. Women and men seemed present in roughly equal numbers; an impression easy enough to confirm, since the sexes had almost without exception congregated on different sides of the room. The occasional interloper peered anxiously through the crowd as if wondering how to reach the appropriate other side of the barrier. The conversation was uneasy, and once in a while a slightly off-balance laugh broke through the murmured undertone. Nodding to a few acquaintances, I settled for a chat with Eleanor, the driving force behind the newsletter for single-parent families.

Gradually the room took on a less edgy appearance. People settled down, either on the few available chairs or balanced on desk tops and windowsills. Aldwyn Potter coughed a few times and then spoke.

'Perhaps we should appoint a chair?'

Somebody from the back suggested him, and he nodded briskly before waving a newspaper in front of him.

'I gather everybody has seen this,' he said.

I said no, and it was passed through the ranks along to me. I stared in amazement.

'Is this a *Telegraph* reading group?' I asked.

'Page six,' Eleanor whispered back, embarrassed.

Aldwyn Potter was being the perfect host; introducing everybody by name as I scanned the article. It was a standard hatchet job, the kind that's appeared twice yearly ever since the Carelton Building got its radical funders. Headed 'Red Refuge Murder', it managed to combine the most gruesome account of Tim's death with a number of unsubstantiated accusations against AER, the trustees of the Foundation, and selected organisations in the building. Bob, the caretaker, was given a minor role, with intimations of his dubious background and concealed hints that the police were investigating his failure to block off a malfunctioning lift.

I'd finished in time to hear what Aldwyn called the last of his introductory remarks.

'... thus, the situation is as follows,' he said. 'One, the police have put Bob into a difficult position, accusing him of negligence. Two, this is the excuse for a witch-hunt by the gutter press that may continue for a considerable time. And, three, the trustees, or certain elements within the Board, may choose to use this unfortunate incident to victimise the less, shall I say — using their words of course — desirable elements within this building.'

11

There were a few nods, but mostly patient stares from those assembled. Finally a woman, perched precariously beside the giant, if ailing, fern, asked,

'So what do you propose we do about it?'

'We at AER suggest that we set up our own investigation,' Aldwyn said, 'with financial backing from all the groups. We, of course, will bear the brunt of the cost. But we would like your support in this venture.'

'Investigation by committee. This tops it all,' muttered a balding man planted in the front ranks.

'No, not by committee. We think it might be an idea to hire an investigator. One of ourselves, somebody who understands the principles by which we work. That is why we invited Kate Baeier to this meeting.'

Twenty heads turned, and forty eyes stared at me. I was flabbergasted.

'Why me?' I managed.

'Because you know us all, you knew Tim, and your work shows you can carry out efficient research,' Aldwyn said. And then added, 'Confidentially.'

'And because you're out of work,' Eleanor contributed.

That was one claim I couldn't deny. Of course, I might be jumping where I couldn't swim. But against that, there was the grim prospect of selling myself over the phone or tedious, imitation French lunches. I agreed to take it on.

That settled, we got to the serious business. The rate at £20 a day, plus expenses, got only a few murmurs of dissent from some anti-technology volunteers, and even from them it was only a token protest. Less easy to decide were the relative contributions of the different groups. Soon ideology took over, with issues of size and funding. Some tried to debate the details of whether charity funding was morally more dispensable than profits from production, but there weren't many takers. I saw a few people getting out their pads and swapping addresses of likely sources of money for diverse projects. But eventually, the passion went out of the discussion. The result was predictable. AER would supply the bulk of my wages, while the rest chipped in for expenses and moral support. I was given ten days to file my initial report ... give or take a few, since with the diaries out, we couldn't agree on a day, let alone an hour.

Finally everybody looked satisfied; all duty done. There were moves towards the door.

'Wait a minute,' I said. 'While you're here, maybe you can all tell me what you know, think or guess about Tim's death.'

'We don't know nothing, lady,' the bald-headed man tried. 'You're the detective.'

'Thanks a lot,' I said. 'I want to know about the lift. How was it possible for Tim to fall? Surely the doors shouldn't have opened if the lift wasn't there.'

'If it was working,' he replied.

'I gather it wasn't?'

'Not for a week,' somebody by the door volunteered. 'It got stuck on the top floor. There were signs on all the doors.'

'I didn't see one on the fourth,' I said.

'So maybe the police took it,' came from within the crowd. Many shrugged. Nobody seemed interested. I let them go, asking, as they filed out, that if anybody could think of anything, they should get in touch.

When they left, they took their energy with them. Intermittent drizzle was still doing its best outside the office: inside, embarrassment hung heavy.

'So what do you think?' I asked. 'Was he pushed or did he fall?'

'This is not time for facetiousness,' Aldwyn snapped.

'No, it isn't. Let's try some information. What do you all think happened?'

They answered simultaneously. From Michael I heard, 'he was drunk'; Aldwyn contributed, 'he killed himself'; and Ron tried, 'what's the difference?'

I was beginning to get angry. 'That's great. Makes my job real easy. If he wasn't killed and he was alone and fell, either deliberately or accidentally, then how will I ever find it out? And if it doesn't matter, what's the point in even trying?'

'It's the note,' Ron stated.

'He left a note?'

'No, the note outside the lift. The one on every floor warning people not to try and use the lift. It wasn't the police who took it. And that's what's giving them their excuse to stir up trouble.'

It was the longest speech I'd managed to get out of Ron for quite a time. I looked at him closely, trying to work out what was bugging him. He had the appearance of someone who'd been keeping late hours and not getting much pleasure from them. Rumours of some tangle between him and Tim's former lover, soon after Ron's girlfriend had proclaimed her pregnancy, echoed in the back of my head, but that's about all they did. I dismissed them and tried another tack.

'Who saw him last?'

Aldwyn stared straight ahead, while a beetroot flush climbed towards his forehead and clashed with his red hair. Ron removed his glasses, gazed at them and then slowly placed them back on his nose. Michael cleared his throat.

'I did,' Michael said. 'We three left together, but I had to come back to pick up some papers. He was busy at his desk and said he would be working late.'

Ron's weak blue eyes were now in focus. 'I think he was meeting somebody. He said something about it when I asked him if he wanted a drink.'

'What was he working on?' I asked.

'South Africa,' Aldwyn said.

'It's a big country,' I tried. No luck. 'Anything special?'

'You know we pay particular attention to South Africa. Tim had a watching brief on it and was preparing some sort of paper. The usual stuff I assume … investments, multinationals, a bit of military activity on the borders. He had been drinking heavily and I assume he was just behind hand,' Aldwyn said. 'It was all routine. You should know about that.'

I nodded. South Africa had been what brought me together with AER in the first place. Somewhere, I think it was at one of those parties where the drink is cheap red and the conversation worse, I'd got talking to a disillusioned PhD student who'd blown the whistle on his chemistry department. He'd gone into postgraduate work with the ideas of science and progress firmly joined in his head, only to discover himself on the bottom end of a military-related production line. He'd dropped out, and was happily tending plants for a London parks department, but on his way he had collected a few rumours that seemed to connect his professor with a hush-hush exchange in South Africa.

It had raised my interest, and I'd done a bit of digging. One of my most interesting assignments, it had lead me to a cocktail party in Oxford. There I'd tried my skills at handing round plates, while assorted academics had talked blithely in front of the help. What they said, when pieced together with snippets of information that I'd gathered from Anti-Apartheid, had added up to a modest engagement by several prominent British academics to line their pockets in South Africa while keeping their images clean. I'd written it up and finally given it to AER, where it fitted neatly into their monthly bulletin. The whole event had made a small dent in the prestige of a few professors and helped selected student groups in their anti-investment campaigns. After that, AER had regularly passed me minor bits of work, which I had undertaken partly to help out, and partly to keep my hand in on developments in Africa.

Through this connection, I'd come to learn a lot about the workings of AER. Started by Michael and Tim on a shoe-string budget, it was one of the good ideas from the early 1970s that hadn't turned into a bad dream by the 1980s. Instead, it had made an impressive leap into financial stability, and the original newsletter had been expanded and divided. Now a monthly business magazine helped pay for the political newsletter which covered developments in Africa.

A respectable organisation with a growing subscription list, AER managed to keep on serviceable terms with the left in Britain and the various solidarity groups that give it muted help while regarding it with faint suspicion. All of this was well known; none of it remotely likely to cause violent death. True, the atmosphere in the office was frequently tense, and few women lasted there fulltime for long. But the men did seem to have settled down to one another's various peculiarities; their social lives only combining at the pub or through some complex bed-hopping. Like I say, it was hardly the setting for murder.

Anyway, I'd taken the job and intended to stick with it for a while. Feeling no point in continuing the questioning session, I left the three to their work and climbed the narrowing stairs to

15

Bob's flat. I rang the bell and then, hearing no sound, knocked on the splintered wood door. It took a long time before I heard footsteps. Finally, the foor opened a crack and Bob peered out. His red-rimmed eyes blinked twice at me.

'Come in,' he said. 'I heard they hired you.'

I was shown through a dingy hall, whose heavy flowered wallpaper contrasted garishly with the hotel-style carpet, and into the sitting-room. The place was spotless, the fake leather three-piece suite lined up with precision. A bottle of Johnny Walker stood on a lace cloth which covered a small table beside one of the chairs. Bob made straight for it and poured himself a slug. With the glass halfway up to his face, he gestured inquiringly at the bottle. I shook my head.

'Rough?' I said.

Bob nodded and then concentrated on his whisky. It was as if time stood still; even the traffic, which resounded throughout the building, seemed to have stopped. From along the hall, I heard a racking cough which rose to a crescendo and then died, as though its originator had lost interest.

'They kept threatening me,' Bob said suddenly. 'Asking why the notice wasn't there and why I hadn't locked Tim out of the building.'

'And did you?' I asked.

He got up as if to protest, but the impulse died halfway. Fixing his eyes on the now empty glass, he nodded. That seemed reason enough for another drink, so he poured one.

I got up and walked slowly to the door. With my hand on the knob, I turned to face him.

'Your mother recovered?' I asked.

Bob shook his head.

'Because I thought she was bed-ridden.'

Again a gesture of the head.

'So you've taken to wearing women's shoes,' I said, pointing to where a pair stuck out, only half hidden by the lace cloth.

Bob might have been hitting the bottle heavily, but that didn't stop his reflexes. He shot up and kicked the shoes from sight.

'I keep them for old times sake,' he muttered.

Feeling slightly sick, I still knew I had to continue.

'I'm not the police, Bob. I don't care who your visitors are. Those shoes are too fashionable to come from the time when your mother could walk.'

'It's not the police, it's him. Yer Lordship.'

'Who runs the building? They're not going to care what your private life is. So you have a friend up here occasionally … so what?'

Bob put down the glass and looked at me for the first time.

'They belong to my sister. The one from the Home. I took her away from it … she wasn't getting any better, and it was a strain visiting her every Sunday. So I thought, why not have her live here. I never asked permission though.'

'It's your flat,' I said.

'Tied to the job though. And I never asked them.'

'So, I won't tell. Was she here on Friday? Is that what the drinking's about?'

I began to feel less of a shit as I saw what looked like relief cross Bob's face. He'd been waiting to tell somebody.

'She acts funny, don't I know that. But then who wouldn't, being where she's been all these years. But she does the odd job for me. Locks the building up, switches off the lights, that type of stuff.'

'And she did it on Friday?'

'It was a special celebration you see, the manager of the Four Crowns retiring with his pile to Worthing, and I wanted to be in on it. So I left her with the keys.'

'And?'

'She likes a kind word. Tim always gave her one, showed that he cared. So when she went to lock up, she left him in the office. He said he was waiting for somebody. She left the door open, and some time later she heard a lot of footsteps and then shouting. She's all right, she is, whatever those social workers say, but she can't stand any violence. Her history you know … I'd kill that husband if he wasn't already dead. So she stayed upstairs and waited. And then when she heard the front door slam, she forgot about it. Only told me on Monday when I found the body.'

'Shouting? Did she hear what it was about?'

'She didn't stick around long enough. Locked herself up in the bathroom. And she said it was a man and a woman, and they

17

sounded like they were ready to kill each other.'

'What about the notice on the lift?'

'It was a long evening,' he said. 'And a lot of drinking. I came back late with the help of some friends. They won't go to the police. But one of them, he runs a fruit-stall down the way, says the lift door was open, so he closed it. He was worried I would fall down. He can't remember the notice, and to tell you the honest truth, I can't remember much. Spent the weekend nursing my hangover and didn't get about. I'd done the shopping on Friday, so I stayed in most of the time. The notice was there on Friday afternoon, that's all I know.

Bob had put the glass down with only one sip gone. The red still ringed his eyes, but some of the old sparkle had returned. I went to the door and this time walked into the hall.

'Thanks a lot,' I said. 'And don't worry, I won't tell anybody about your sister.'

I went downstairs and was almost at the bottom when I remembered my hat. A giant notice proclaimed the lift still out of action, so I took to my feet and up to the fourth. Outside the door, the sound of raised voices made me pause.

' ... we have to tell her.' It was Aldwyn's voice. 'If he was working on something significant, and you all know that I doubt that.'

'It's a red herring,' Michael shouted. 'And what's the point of getting her involved?'

'In what?' I said, stepping in. 'And do I have the honour of being she?'

They whipped round at me, both mouths agape.

'It's nothing, Kate,' Aldwyn said sulkily. 'Just some work problems.'

'Tell me another,' I said.

Michael turned on the charm. And he could be charming in a sort of good-looking little boy way, when he wasn't playing the Big Chief Sitting Bull role.

'It really is nothing, Kate,' he said. 'Just that Tim was working on something he considered very special and we were wondering whether to tell you. On the face of it, it doesn't seem very important.'

'Let me judge,' I said.

'Argentina ,' he said. 'Tim said he'd found something.'

'I thought he was working on South Africa?'

Aldwyn and Michael exchanged an exasperated look that they didn't want me to miss.

'Haven't you heard the rumours?' Michael asked, gently.

'Which particular ones? I did hear one the other day about Red Rulers closing up, but my source was so unreliable he could have been referring to the time they went bankrupt only to discover that the bookkeeper had done their sums wrong and it was all a ghastly mistake. I also heard one about … '

Michael interrupted. 'The rumours about Argentina and South Africa co-operating on a top secret project.'

'Oh, that rumour,' I said. 'Silly me, that's been doing the rounds for quite a time.'

'Well, that's it,' Michael said.

'That's it? What's it? Or to put it another way, why is it it ?'

'Tim was working on it and said he'd found something.'

Aldwyn had had enough. 'I never believed it anyway. Tim always did have a conspiracy view of politics. Nobody here ever got to find out what he was so excited about. Did they Michael?'

Aldwyn lost interest and he turned away even before Michael came through with his short 'no'. I found myself facing two backs: too busy backs that weren't much interested in spinning this one out any further. I gave up.

'Tim had money, didn't he?' I tried. 'I mean an awful lot of it?'

'You're already getting paid,' Aldwyn sneered.

I ignored that, except to say sharply, 'Even you should be able to see that maybe somebody stands to benefit by his death. I'd always gathered he wasn't paid by AER because he had a private income.'

'He inherited from his father. I don't know how much, but it was a lot. All of it, so that his mother got nothing. I know he had to make a will so that she wouldn't get it if he died first. He didn't like to talk about it,' Michael said.

'Do you know who his lawyers are?' I asked.

They pretended to search through their memories, neither of them very convincingly. Finally, Aldwyn let me off the hook.

'Quick … no, Slick and Stevens — that's it. Tim always joked about a Bond Street solicitor with that on his headed notepaper,' he said.

'And now, if there is nothing more?' Michael asked.

Outside, I searched for a phone box — or, to put it more accurately, I found several phone boxes, one jammed, one decapitated and one just plain difficult, before I managed to speak to Slick. Robert Slick it was, and his phone manner matched his name. He agreed to set up a date for the next day. Tim's name obviously still had the ability to open the gilt doors of fancy law firms.

It was getting late for lunch, and my stomach knew it. I took a walk to Poons and ordered a noodle soup along with a side dish of garlic fried greens. While I ate, my mind stayed a pleasant blank.

I wandered over to Old Compton Street, bought a bottle of Armagnac and a pound of fresh ground mocha, and then for a couple of hours played about with the idea of acquiring garments of various colours and purposes. It never got to the stage where money changed hands. It was basic diversionary activity, heightened only by a periodic feeling that somebody was following me. After a while I stopped looking over my shoulder and put the feeling down to a hangover from the days in Portugal, where being tailed had been an everyday hazard.

By six I was slipping my key into the door of Anna and Daniel's ever-welcome house. Anna and I had met in the most unlikely of places — an aeroplane, mid-Atlantic and buffeted by what the pilot called a stiff breeze. When he had called it that for the fifth time, I was poker still, gripping at the arm rests. Keeping a plane up requires concentration, and so I was barely conscious of the woman beside me who appeared to be involved in detailed monologue about the weather. It was a good hour before I realised that she wasn't talking about the breezes but instead about the Weather Underground. I'd joined in and become so involved that I had forgotten about my flying phobia: it was only later I learned that conversation was Anna's way of dealing with hers.

By the time the plane landed, Anna and I had discovered that we had more in common than phobias. We both hated the English upper middle class, over-cooking, and health foods, and we loved Hollywood matinées, Remy Martin, massages and the thought of saunas. We were both aliens in the country. She was an

American who'd married English, divorced soon, but had stayed in her job as a film editor with the BBC. When she'd lost her job in one of the corporation's purges of the early 1970s, she'd gone freelance. Now she made a good living by working under her former colleagues, whose liberal commitments had shrunk as their status had grown.

It might have been the end of nothing more than a memorable plane ride, if Daniel hadn't been there to meet her. Another American, Daniel was historian who'd come to London University on a sabbatical, got bored with academic life, and became a stringer for several American newspapers. He specialised in labour relations and managed to slip in left-wing analysis under the guise of educating the American public about Britain. He and I had been going to the same union meetings for some time, had smiled across the room at each other, but had never got to talking.

They'd given me a lift, and over the weeks, we'd all upped the contact, until their house had become my second home. We made an easy threesome, and when Sam had come along, he'd been quickly accepted into the scene.

That Tuesday I walked into the house and nearly got blasted out again. This must have been a boring day for them. They'd turned on every machine to compensate. The dishwasher and baby gagia were competing to see which could supply the most steam. Anna's video was playing some gory American cop scene, to the tune of 'It's My Party And I'll Cry If I Want To', which was blaring from the stereo. Sam was shouting, either in anger or to hear his own voice, over the phone.

As I stepped into the large light living-room the noise miraculously stopped. The dishwasher ended its cycle and Daniel finished making the last cappuccino, as Sam shouted his good-byes to the party on other end of the line. Anna, who was lying stretched out on the couch, a rug draped over her legs, moved her eyelids a millimetre to acknowledge my presence.

' "The Streets of San Francisco" at this time of day?' I said. 'Things are really deteriorating around here.'

Daniel started talking about the latest NUJ meeting. I tried to follow the complications of the in-fighting, but stopped concentrating as Sam began a cross conversation about geometric images

21

in landscape poetry.

I accepted a cup of coffee and went to sit opposite Anna. She wasn't looking her best. Her job had been forcing her into midnight sessions with irascible directors, and the circles under her large brown eyes showed it. Her hair had changed again: she'd gone, this time, for a modern look, with the brown curls pulled away from her small face and piled straight up on her head. By the look of dissatisfaction on her face, it wasn't going to stay that way for long.

'I've got a new job,' I announced.

'Don't tell me, they're going to run a series based on that article about tropical legumes as a world food source,' Sam said. 'Or that multinational you slammed on the size of its calculator has been so inundated with complaints that it's buying you off with a fortune.'

'Detection,' I said. 'I've been hired by AER to investigate Tim's death.'

All they could manage was a long hard stare.

'I thought he fell,' Daniel said at last.

'So did I. And there's no evidence that he didn't. But they hired me just to see. I'm not exactly sure why. They're using police intimidation and caretaker victimisation as the excuse. But the way that they're behaving says something else. Nobody's going out of the way to help me. Still, it's a job and I might as well try it out. Who knows, it might lead to a new career. What do you all think?'

'You do need a change, I suppose,' Sam said.

'And this might be interesting,' said Anna. 'Plus, I've got the latest from my producer. You know, the one who had a brief fling with Michael. Said she couldn't stand the pace and the hard drinking, but what completely threw her was what she calls their lack of containment. In the bed department, that is. She discovered that Ron is having his second affair with Barbara Sloan, who was first Michael's and then Tim's girlfriend. She also happens to be one of Rhoda's best friends,' Anna said.

'Rhoda? Who's Rhoda?' Daniel always finds it difficult to follow the gossip that Anna and I have as a sort of private language. We ran through our routine: giving him a house-by-house summary of the Dalston/Islington nexus, so that he could place Rhoda. By the time we'd finished, Daniel's eyes had taken on a glazed appearance and we were having to put up with heavy heckling from Sam's direction.

We were saved from acrimony by the phone. Daniel went to answer it as I gazed outside. Just at its end, the day was rescuing itself. An orange sunset shone throught the leafy branches of a solitary oak; a sparkling summer setting replaced the wet, gray monotony. As the peace of it was beginning to settle within me, Daniel called me to the phone. Annoyed, I got up and mouthed a brisk hello.

'Kate Baeier?' He had an abrupt South African accent and a phone manner to match it. 'We have to meet.'

'That's a proposal I might just be able to resist. Who are you and how did you get this number?' I said.

'That's none of your business. I know plenty. Meet me at AER at ten tomorrow.'

His instruction had a ring of finality, so I jumped in quickly.

'Sorry, can't make it. I have a previous appointment. How about eleven?'

'You be there,' he said.

I put the phone down, slowly trying to identify the voice while it was still fresh in my ears. I didn't get far. I have an accurate aural memory and I was pretty sure that the caller didn't mix in the most public of South African exile circles. His accent was strong; strong enough for me to guess that he couldn't have reached England too early in his life. But it was also muted in the way that distinguishes white English-speaking South Africans from their Afrikaans counterparts.

I described the call to the others and we played around with it, trying to work out what it all meant. Nobody thought of much to contribute, and so after a while Anna and Daniel turned their attention to our meal. By eight we'd got through two bottles of Barbeira d'Alba, which had matched perfectly the home-made spaghetti Bolognese and fresh green salad. Lethargy set in as we talked sporadically, with only Daniel animated by his grandiose plan for a new international writers' union. After a couple of hours,

Sam and I were ready to go home, and it only took a brief negotiation to decide on his flat.

As we entered the door, the phone was ringing. I reached for it. Silence. A slight buzz resounded in the background, interrupted by the faint echo of heavy breathing. I handed the phone to Sam.

'It's Matthew,' I said.'

'What's he doing up?' Sam muttered, his slight irritation combined with a smattering of parental concern.

They talked for about ten minutes. Finally, Sam put the phone down with a grin on his face.

'So, what's he doing up so late?' I asked.

'He phoned to tell me he was going to be sick.'

'Margaret must have been pleased. Was she hovering with a basin in the background?'

'Not that sort of sick,' he said. 'He's going to be sick tomorrow. When I told him I couldn't be around, he decided he'd got the dates mixed up and was really going to be sick on Thursday. He thinks he's developing something that sounds like slotinitis.'

'Things not going well at the nursery?'

'He said it was disgusting and horrible and that John gave him a Bounty, Miss Whitney gave him a Milky Way and told him to wash his hands, and … '

'Okay, I get the picture. So you're having him Thursday?'

'Might as well,' he said. 'Can't have him giving the other kids slotinitis. It's bad for the image.'

Sam got out the whisky, and we lay in bed drinking as we watched a 1950s thriller where the well-coiffed women acted surprised to counterbalance the men's rumpled hairstyles and tough exteriors.

Halfway through, we got bored and turned it off. I fell asleep wondering whether the disarrayed lock of hair on the brunette's head was a clue to her part in the second murder or just an indication of her shimmering sexuality. Probably the two were synonymous, but I daresay this will remain one of the unsolved mysteries in my life.

3.

'How about this one?' I asked.

Sam nodded without much conviction and turned back to his coffee. I couldn't blame him. One of the problems of living in two separate flats was the mismatch of clothes divided between them. The weather — bright, sunny and promising to climb well over the last week's low sixties — had caught me unawares. With no time to return home, I spent a lot of energy trying for the right image to pay a call on the lawyers. In the end, I settled for a pair of red culottes and a green blouse that didn't clash too badly with my multi-coloured espadrilles. There would be no way Slick and Stevens could ignore me, I thought, as I took the tube to Bond Street.

After twenty minutes of waiting in the subtle brown-upholstered chair, I wasn't so sure. An impression of solid money was neatly stamped on the whole room. The walls lined with expensively bound law books added weight to the half-drawn velvet curtains and the not quite new, but certainly well-hoovered mustard carpet. Snappily dressed young couriers wandered in and out, exchanging pleasantries with the receptionist, who managed a few smiles between her phoning and filing. Otherwise she was a study in cool efficiency. Only when a young black woman catapulted herself from a side door into the room, did she allow herself a disapproving frown.

'Miss Jones,' she enunciated carefully. 'That won't do. We walk sedately.'

A look of contempt crossed the woman's face as she walked slowly and deliberately towards the receptionist.

'Sure thing, Lisa,' she called.

'And please lower your voice, Miss Jones. As you can see, we have a client waiting.'

The rest of the conversation was muffled. I tried to eavesdrop, but without success.

One thing was plain: whatever they were arguing about, Miss

Jones wasn't on the winning side. The impression of energy she'd brought with her evaporated under the relentless pressures of her interrogation. She kept shaking her head, but the conviction in her denials was gradually replaced by worry. Once they both looked in my direction, but with a meaning I couldn't fathom.

It was 9.45 when the intercom buzzed. The receptionist raised her voice and pointed it in my direction.

'Mr Slick will see you now. Up the stairs, turn right, and his office is at the end of the corridor.'

I padded upstairs, found the room, knocked and walked in. Robert Slick was seated behind a stained-wood desk. My first impression was that he was a small man, but as my eyes adjusted, I changed my mind. He looked small, I realised, because of the sheer scale of his office. Downstairs had been business-like rich, but this was sumptuous. One corner was occupied by a rounded sculpture that could only have been a Henry Moore. The gray carpet was deep pile, the embossed wallpaper saved from vulgarity by the subtlety of design. The light was muted despite the three full-length windows that admitted no sound.

Robert Slick, I discovered, when I got closer, was by no means small. Dressed in a well-fitting black suit, a gray-pink shirt that toned with his thick gray hair, and a thin black tie that was almost the height of fashion, he exuded an air of confidence as he gestured me to the chair in front of his desk. He paused awhile, waiting for me to get my breath back and settle into a proper respect for him. His voice when he spoke was almost mellow, but with a practised resonance of authority.

'Miss Baeier. Good of you to come. I understand you can shed some light on Mr Nicholson's unfortunate demise.' His sentences hung in the air until they were ready to leave.

'I'm investigating it,' I said. 'And would like some information from you.'

His eyebrows rose a fraction. 'Of what nature, may I ask?'

'I'm interested in who benefits financially from his death.'

This time the eyebrows stayed put, but a disapproving frown hung above them.

'Surely you know we are unable to release such information?' he stated.

26

'Even if it would help find out how he died?'

The frown deepened. It was distinctly disapproving.

'We have been informed by the police that it was an accident. I see no reason to doubt their word. Now, if that is all … ?'

He half rose and pointed to the door. I got up and walked towards it. My hand was on the smooth brass knob before he spoke again.

'Thank you so much for this visit,' he said. 'I am sorry I could not be of assistance to you in your … activities. I'm sure you will not do so, but perhaps if you do come across certain legal documents at Mr Nicholson's work premises, you could inform me?'

'What's the matter,' I said. 'Lost the will?'

His bland front was momentarily disturbed by an almost evil look. He replaced it quickly and nodded pleasantly. I stepped out. As I walked down the corridor a door opened slightly. I glanced in. A harassed man, his top shirt button open, was picking through a mass of paper that threatened to engulf his tiny office.

Outside I collected my thoughts. They weren't worth that much. I was just about to leave when the door opened and a woman came rushing out. I stepped to intercept her and she catapulted into me.

'Oh shit,' she said. 'This sure isn't my day.'

'Miss Jones. Just the person I was thinking of.'

She threw me a look deep with suspicion.

'On whose account?' she said.

'Mine. Just wondered whether you know anything about Tim Nicholson's will.'

This time she looked disgusted.

'Not you, too. If you don't mind, I've got to post these letters.'

I reached for her elbow.

'Get your hands off,' she said. 'Anyway, how do you know my name?'

'I heard the frozen receptionist trying to get you to conform.'

She smiled. 'Like that, is it? But I can't help you. It's more than my job's worth. And maybe I am just a race relations tool for those …' she left it in the air while her eyes said it. 'But at least I get paid. The way my kids burn up the money, that's not nothing.'

'Did you lose it? The will, that is,' I asked.

'Don't give me none of that. I'll get the blame in the end, because who's going to believe me over Slicksy. But I know he took it away. I know, even though old Robert didn't notate it. They call me a liar because in that place, what Robert doesn't notate never happened. Now excuse me,' she removed my hand and walked off.

I started in the other direction. I'd only got a few yards when I felt a hand on my elbow.

'Ask Mrs Nicholson,' she said.

'His mother?'

'No, his wife.' And with that she was off.

By the time I'd reached the Carelton Building, I still hadn't come to terms with it. Tim Nicholson had been born into an upper-class background which had plenty of history and the money to back it up, but not much emotion. Radicalised in the 1960s, he'd renounced his background and thrown his efforts towards the left. From what I'd heard, his family, or parts of it that hadn't already died by gun or drink, didn't approve. But there had been money for him all the same. And clearly more than he had led me to suppose. Still, even then, he had been guilty about it, unable either to accept or turn his back on it. He'd settled on an uneasy compromise of good living combined with a defensiveness that swayed between meanness and open-handed generosity.

He had tried to talk about the conflict. I'd heard a lot about his family and the rift between his mother and father, his fear and humiliation during his public school days, and the final break with his background. But despite his apparent frankness, Tim had never mentioned a wife.

Halfway up the stairs, I bumped into Bob. Or to be more accurate, I fell right over him. By the look of the colour in his cheeks Bob had recovered his equanimity, but his behaviour didn't seem exactly standard. He was kneeling, his ear pressed against a keyhole.

'Smell that,' he said.

'Smell what?'

'Ssh,' he whispered. 'I've almost caught them at it.'

'Uhuh,' I whispered back.

'It's AAAT. I've got them at it. I told them about the fire regulations ... no electric appliances without permission, and now I think

28

they're frying eggs on a burner.'

Bob's battles with the Alliance Against Advanced Technology were legendary. Nobody had ever been able to explain just why he chose to feud with them. Certainly they were so inconvenienced that they were always trying to conciliate him. It had been Bob who'd produced a by-law of the building, declaring that no bicycles could be kept in the entrance hall; as a result, successive volunteers struggled up the steps to place their bicycles where they could trip up unsuspecting visitors. Now it looked like Bob had reached a new phase in his vendetta.

'Anybody waiting for me upstairs?' I asked.

'Nope. No one there at all. I did hear somebody earlier, but then I smelt the eggs.'

I continued my journey upwards. Just before I was about to round the stairs, Bob's voice reached me.

'Thanks for everything, Kate,' he said, before he bent back to his door.

The AER offices were open and, as Bob had said, empty of people. But that wasn't all. Whereas the day before, Tim's desk had displayed the habitual disorder that had been his working hallmark, now it looked as though it had been hit by a bomb. Somebody had been searching and had done a thorough job.

I moved to the desk and desultorily began to pick through the remains. Like many in his field, Tim had designed a filing system that seemed to defy all logic. I'd once tried to penetrate it when I was after a particular file, but with no luck. I'd begun to think that Tim just filed for appearance's sake, but when he'd arrived he'd dug out what I wanted within a few seconds. Now, newspaper clippings, odd bits of hand-written scrawl and exerpts from articles lay around haphazardly. I flipped through them, but they all seemed like standard items. It was only when I decided to be more methodical and shake what was apparently a pile of empty folders, that I produced anything even vaguely interesting. A scrap of paper floated to the ground. I picked it up and puzzled over it. Printed on both sides, it had been cut out of a semi-glossy magazine. By the look of the typeface, it had first seen life in the back pages of *Street Times*. On one side was an invitation for applicants to write to the GLC , County Hall, quoting a reference number SLD

2345. On the other, was what looked like an ad from the lonely hearts columns.

'Male, brown eyes, Pisces,' it read, 'seeks squash companion.'

I folded the paper and stuck it in my bag before I continued my search. It was half eleven before I heard a voice behind me.

'Searching Tim's desk?'

I jumped, and turned, and then relaxed with relief.

'Hi, Ron. No, I'm just looking. Somebody else did the search.'

Ron Critchley tried a nod which became a movement into coffee-making. That took time, since first the milk and then the sugar had gone missing. But by twelve we were seated, with mugs in our hands.

'What's up? Been keeping late hours?' I asked.

He gave me a wry smile. He took a few sips from his mug, and this seemed to revive him.

'I'm everybody's punching bag,' he said. 'Rhoda shouts at me because I'm having an affair. And Barbara shouts at me because Rhoda's angry and she doesn't think I've been straight with her. And my household is after my blood for not doing the housework, which I can't do because everybody shouts at me.'

'So, why are you doing it.'

'Oh Kate, don't you start. Who's been at Tim's desk?'

'No idea. I was supposed to meet somebody here, but he never turned up. I just found the office like this. Did you know that Tim had a wife?'

Ron's glasses stopped in mid-air.

'A what?' he asked.

'A wife. You know … marriage, white dresses, family rows, bourgeois institution and all that. Did Tim have a wife?'

'Not that I ever heard of. Why?'

'Just something somebody said. Would Tim have kept his will here?'

'How should I know. I doubt it.' Ron hesitated. It took a time before he could find the words. 'Have you found anything about South Africa?'

'Only the usual stuff. What did you expect?'

Again hesitation. 'Just an idea,' he said.

'So, share it with me.'

The hesitation had gone. Ron had reached a decision.

'No, it's just a crazy idea. No point in spreading rumours,' he said.

As far as he was concerned, that was the end of the conversation. I brought out the cutting.

'Have you ever seen this?'

Ron glanced at it. 'Looks like a lonely hearts. You're getting desperate. Are you sure you wouldn't like to turn to women? I've got two I need help with.'

'Bad taste, Ron,' I said. 'Where do you keep the *Street Times?*'

He got up and opened the door of the walk-in cupboard that stored many of the free magazines that arrived through some out-of-control exchange system. He looked once, and then more carefully.

'That's funny,' he said, 'they're gone. Why would anyone want to take them?'

'That's not the only question I'd like answered. Were you planning to come in this late today?'

'Yes. We've met this month's deadline, and we all decided to give ourselves some time off. Why?'

'Because somebody searched Tim's desk, and I wondered how he knew nobody would be here.'

'Maybe he wouldn't have done it if we had been.'

'Maybe,' I said. 'I'm going. Catch you later.'

I strolled through the Brewer Street market, buying a few of the items that caught my eye. By the time I arrived at the bus stop, I'd acquired two bunches of asparagus, some fennel with the leaves still attached, and a pound of fresh pasta from Lena's. I had plenty of time to stare at them while I waited for the 38. When it arrived, I climbed on and sat next to two children who were pretending to be one. On the way we discussed school meals, which didn't sound like they'd significantly improved since my time, and then played an anarchic game of 'I Spy'.

The bus finally made it to Dalston, and I got off and sauntered through the last five minutes to my home. The outside door was open but I didn't really take much notice of it. Instead, I climbed the two flights, slipped my key through my front door and walked into my work room. There I halted, and stared. The mess hadn't gone away, but something else had been added.

On the floor, stretched out and still, lay a man. A man I had never seen before and who looked as though no one, except for those people who deal with bodies would ever see him again. My first feeling was fury. This is why I gave up communal living, I thought, just so I wouldn't have to come home and find strange men lying dead on my floor.

Who knows how long I could have gone on with this chain of thought if I hadn't heard the noise from my bedroom. It's the cat, I thought, a reassurance which lasted the few seconds before I realised I didn't have one. After that, adrenalin took over. I rushed out and into my car; and by the time that my rational mind emerged from its hiding place, I was banging on the door in Cardozo Road. Sam answered.

'What are you doing here?' I asked.

'What's the matter?' he said.

'What are you doing here?'

Sam took in the situation and decided that the best policy was to answer.

'I'm discussing a pamphlet on poetic metaphors in contemporary film with Anna,' he said. 'Come in and tell me what's happened.'

I was led to a sofa where I sat awhile before I could find any words. When I did, they came rushing out.

'There's a dead man in my flat. And somebody else making noises. It's not the cat. I checked my memory on that and remembered I didn't have one. But the man's still dead and the other one … '

I ran out of words. When Anna and Daniel came in, I repeated my story more slowly, It didn't make better sense that way, but it was more relaxing on the jaw. Then we all sat around, with not a clue of what to do next.

'Let's go over there,' Anna said suddenly.

That was the signal we'd been waiting for. We piled into Anna's red Citroen and drove to Dalston. We arrived clutching the weapons that Daniel had assembled before we left. I was allocated a spade. Daniel clasped a garden fork which looked incongruous against Sam's hammer. Anna was brandishing what looked suspiciously like a poker but turned out to be a knife sharpener.

In front of the house our bravado evaporated: we hesitated. From across the street, three Rastas put down the bulky speakers they'd been moving and stared across at us. A knot of people gathered around them. It began as a silent vigil; but as the seconds ticked by, questions darted from the crowd. A young man detached himself from the mass and walked confidently across the road. It was Rodney, a neighbour from two doors down.

'Hey Kate,' he said. 'What's happening?'

'Strangers in my flat,' I said. 'And we're ... '

I froze. From inside the house came the sound of a door slowly closing. Halting footsteps echoed down the hall. We all moved a step backwards as the gap in the front door began to widen. A hand appeared. Three bottles were placed on the top step. The crowd gasped. Another hand joined it: this time it placed a note in one of the bottles. The crowd laughed, clapped and then started to disperse.

Hearing the noise, Greta stepped out, blinking into the sunlight.

'Hello there,' she said. 'Did you forget your keys?'

'Keys? The door was open,' I grimaced. This woman was weird. Always eccentric of dress, she had excelled herself. Her hairdresser had made an attempt at a modern cut: the effect was disastrous. Tufts of fair hair sprang from her scalp, overwhelming the garish hair grips that she'd stuck on either side. She was wearing a dress that had started out life as a demure black number, complete with white cuffs and collar. Age, and Greta, had ensured that instead of giving off an air of respectability, it looked almost slovenly. She had tried to pull the image back into line by wearing a sedate pair of black patent leather shoes, but the fishnet white stockings with their suspiciously large holes meant that she didn't really have a chance.

My downstairs neighbour and something of a recluse, Greta always faced the world with a bewildered expression. Four people planted aggressively on her doorstep were just another of the unexplained mysteries in her life. Any minute now, she would launch into one of the tirades in which she specialised. I think she used them to fill the gaps between the various incidents in her life.

'Kate,' she said. 'I'm glad we met. I've been meaning to ask you to tread more softly. I've had insomnia and was trying to rest this afternoon when I heard a loud banging from above.'

'I wasn't in. Must have been from next door,' I said, trying to get through the doorway.

Greta wouldn't give up. 'No, it was from your flat. I know because my photograph of the yellow freesia, the one I took in France in '74 — you know, the one that I blew up at Sky — moved this afternoon, and it always does that when there are vibrations of the ceiling. I've worked out that it's the centre light swinging which creates a breeze.'

'Well, I'm sorry. There seems to have been a little action in my flat, and I bet it was noisy. Somebody was killed there. You probably heard a murder. What time was it?'

Greta's face didn't change. 'Shit,' she said. 'I'm going to miss the nineteen minutes past. I'll have to run.' And, shutting the door, she took off down the road.

The conversation had been enough to wipe away my fear. And by the incredulous looks on the faces of the others, Greta had done the same for them.

I opened the door, and we climbed the stairs two at a time. Through the wall came the half-smothered sounds of an electric guitar. The man next door was at it again, playing what sounded like repetitive bars of flamenco music. If persistence was any guide, he would go far — although his choice of music often made me wonder where exactly he was headed.

At the top I opened the door to my flat and, my hand gripping Anna's for reassurance, walked into the living-room. Things had changed, but only marginally for the better. The room was still a mess. But now at least there was no dead man on the floor, and, by the sounds of relief from Daniel and Sam, no live person in any other room.

There was also no glass in the window overlooking the garden, and no sign of even the hasty order I'd imposed the previous Monday. My papers were scattered everywhere. The place looked like it had been the object of someone's fantasy mission to destroy. And then, after a brief check, came the final blow.

'Oh no,' I shouted. 'I've had it. How could they do this?'

Anna came rushing over. 'What's happened? Did you find some blood?'

'Worse than that. My saxophone is gone.'

I felt ready to kill. It had taken me months of tracking dead-end ads to find the alto; I'd repadded, resprung and polished it until it gleamed. Of all my possessions, it was the most precious.

I slumped down into the deepest armchair and stared moodily in front of me, flicking Sam's hand away when he tried to console me. No one spoke for a while.

'What do you say? Should we try the cops?'

I shrugged. 'What's the good? It's gone.'

'Come on Kate, its … ' Anna began.

'How do you know? It's not your alto,' I snapped and then retreated back into the curve of my misery.

When I looked up again, they were all watching me. 'What's so interesting? Why don't you all go do something … ' I stopped. I had nothing to suggest.

'It's awful,' Anna said.

'What am I going to do?' I wailed. 'I can't get another alto. And I'm scared.'

'It's all right, we're with you now,' Sam said. 'Maybe we should report the missing alto to the police. It's easily recognisable. So even if it's an outside chance, maybe we should try it.'

'But what about the body? Do we tell them about that, too?' Anna asked.

We swapped confused looks. For four people who had very little good to say about the police, we were in a no-win game. We didn't believe they could do anything, but then we certainly weren't used to dealing with disappearing bodies ourselves.

'I think we should,' I said. 'If things get worse, we may as well have it all on record.'

It seemed like as good a reason an any. Anna wandered into the kitchen to pour us all a drink and then dialled the Dalston police station. She finally got through and started off bright and charming. Within minutes, her expression had deteriorated into one of pure exasperation, and she was having a lot of difficulty controlling her temper.

'Mine's Huebsch, HUEBSCH, but her surname is Baeier, BAEIER. No, not with a 'y'. No there's no 't' either. Let me spell it again,' we heard her enunciating into the receiver.

That was only the beginning. Anna can be a smooth operator

and she pitched her story to get maximum credibility. On the grounds that break-ins are ordinary business, three a block on a good day, she described the alto theft first. The desk sergeant was able to cope with that one, even if, from the sounds of the gaps in his side of the conversation, he could hardly raise enough interest to fill out his forms. In the end, though, Anna's attempts to prepare him for the sticky part of the story didn't help. When she started on the disappearing dead man, she was interrupted at every turn.

Finally, she managed to interrupt the stream of doubts coming from the other end. 'Sure I see your problem,' she said, 'you don't believe me. But how am I supposed to know where he went? I'd hardly keep that information from you deliberately. Still, if you're not interested, forget it.'

She listened awhile, a smile creeping onto her face. Finally the conversation ended, and she turned to us.

'They're coming round. At one point they just wanted to get me off the line, but as soon as I acted uninterested in them they got keen again. Just like the police.'

We settled down to wait. By the time that the door bell rang, I'd drunk two vodka-and-tonics: they helped to blur the unpleasant side of life without my alto. I went to the intercom, got nothing more than a burst of static, and pressed the red release button.

I waited at the top of the stairs for PC 359 to appear. The police had gone for a compromise: they'd acted quickly and sent someone round, but he looked a shade inexperienced. Fresh-faced and uneasy, he had adopted the stern face of the beginner policeman, trying to be tough. His name didn't make him any more impressive: PC Jones, he introduced himself.

'And you are Miss Bates,' he stated in a flat monotone.

I sighed. 'The name's Baeier. Come in, and I'll show you where it happened.

I led him into the sitting-room. My friends greeted him with a combination of half hellos and measuring looks. I know that when they're dealing with authority, they can be quite imposing. I would have felt sorrier for him, if he hadn't acted so stiff. He managed to ignore them at the same time as he flushed under his thin layer of acne. He must have known how bad this looked, because he tried to cover it up by doing a quick inspection of the room and curtly refusing my offer of a chair. Finally, he turned on his full five foot ten and a half inches and faced me resolutely. I sat down.

He looked uneasy when he spoke. 'I understand that you reported a break-in and entry to the Dalston Lane police station. Could you supply me with the details of the missing possessions?' He took out his notebook with a studied, if unconvincing, air of official concern.

'Just my alto and the glass from my windows, as far as I've noticed. Unless of course you count the missing corpse as a possession.'

He stared at me. 'We'll be looking into the matter of the reputed disappearance of an unknown person in due course. For the moment, please answer my questions. I need to get the sequence of events right so that we have a correct statement.'

'Well, then, you'd better listen to me,' I said. 'For a start, the dead man appeared first.' I reached for my drink.

'Wait a minute,' Sam said. 'That's what we've been assuming. But ... ' he lifted his finger to emphasise a smart point '... the murderer might have been waiting for him.'

I thought about that and rejected it. 'I can't see it. Your version makes it all too carefully planned. If the murderer was here first, then the murderer knew he was going to kill the murderee and, what's more, knew that the murderee was coming here. I prefer the possibility that the murderer followed the murderee.'

'Aha, but how do you know he was dead?' Anna said. 'Remember we haven't spotted any blood.'

'And why in your flat?' Daniel added. 'You didn't know this man, and you probably didn't know the murderer. So what was either of them doing here?'

'And if he was dead, who carried him out?' Sam contributed. 'And why?'

I just had to put a stop to this before they went round the circle again.

'What am I supposed to be − a detective?' I snapped.

'Yes,' all three smugly chanted.

I shrugged that off. 'All right, give me a chance. One case at a time. I know for sure that the dead man wasn't Tim. He's dead already.'

That shut them up. PC Jones, still standing where he'd planted himself, had begun to rock from foot to foot. He looked unhappy.

'Please leave the disappearance of the murderee ...' he stumbled into a dead end. He tried to look menacing, but tried was the operative word. I wasn't impressed. He pulled himself together and tried again.

'Miss Baxter,' he shouted.

'Baeier,' I said. 'I'm warning you, I can take only so much alteration of my name.'

The police soldiered on. 'I'd like to inspect the rest of your flat.'

'Go ahead,' I answered. 'If you're looking for the bathroom, it's second on the right.'

This time, I only saw the back of his neck go red. He did a perfectly executed turn and walked out.

There was a short pause before Anna spoke. 'I've worked out what's going on,' she said in a stage whisper that would have had no problem in reaching a ticket collector outside a crowded auditorium.

'He's too green. How can you take him seriously − a policeman not yet out of his adolescence.'

'Well, who knows,' Daniel answered. 'Maybe there's been a glut of maniacs killing men and stealing saxophones and they're bored with it all, so they send a kid in blue to deal with it.'

As he finished, the kid walked back in. They must be teaching breathing techniques to the police these days, because he had calmed himself down and didn't even blush. He managed to avoid his old spot on the floor and instead sat down opposite me. He also remembered to leave my name out of it. He stared hard to get my attention.

'What else is missing?' he asked.

'Just the cigar cutter.'

'Wait a minute. You reported a missing instrument.'

'It was a cigar cutter Selmer alto,' I said.

'You know I've never understood why it was called that,' Daniel mused.

'It's the thumb rest. The mother-of-pearl button's got a dent in the middle and the two sides slope towards the dent. Looks like a cigar cutter,' I said.

'And is it articulated?' Daniel asked.

'Sure − it's the second one in the modern range, I think. It is, I mean it was, a good instrument.'

PC Jones had kept his head busy moving from Daniel to me and back again throughout the exchange and he was having difficulty stopping it. It was obvious that he wanted to escape.

'Do you have any enemies?' he said, his arms already pushing himself upright.

'No one I know would go to the extent of getting a corpse here and then have the excess energy to remove it.'

'And that's exactly why I don't think he's dead,' Anna said.

Jones and I ignored her. He rose to go. I tried to follow.

'Don't bother, I'll show myself out,' he said. 'I'll report this.'

He left, trailing his dignity behind him. Silence. I was feeling strangely detached: the combination of corpse and inept policeman on a summer's day was so unlikely that I'd filed it all away under the category of useless noise. Only when I thought of my alto did I feel the twinge of panic.

The others seemed to have plain run out of words. After a short time, we set to work on the mess. This was the second time in two days, but it was a lot easier with company. We made a good combination, working fast without getting in one another's way. By the end of half an hour, we'd achieved a lot.

Even the phone was easy to find when it rang.

'Kate Baeier?'

'Yes, who is it?

'Never you mind. We have your saxophone. If you want to see it again, then come to the end of Ridley Road in an hour.'

I gestured wildly to the room, while I racked my brains for something to say.

'Why are you doing this?' was all I could manage.

'Meet me in an hour,' the voice repeated.

My voice sounded light in comparison. 'Which end of Ridley Road?' I asked. 'Anyway, I thought you said meet us. You on your own now?'

'I ... just be there. Kingsland Road end.' The dialling tone echoed in my ears.

I put the phone down. I wasn't feeling too good. The voice had seemed familiar, but I couldn't connect it to a face. I wasn't sure whether that made it more or less creepy. One thing I did know. Things were getting out of hand.

'We'll have to go with it. See what happens next,' Sam said.

'So how are we going to fill the next hour?' I asked.

'Let's go shopping,' Anna said. 'I've got this neat route worked out. We can pass that pair of shoes I've been wanting to show you and drop in on the stationers to pick up a few boxes of the new felt tips. Then if we buy the coffee quickly, we'll be back at Ridley Road in good time.'

Anna and I headed for the door, while Daniel and Sam tried rear guard prevention. Daniel went into a coherent attack on the evils of consumerism, but we stopped his flow by getting Sam to admit that his own reaction was tempered with jealousy.

By five to six, I had bought nothing, and Anna had already returned a cheap bag that had had an astonishingly short lifespan. We arrived at the corner of Ridley and Kingsland Road to find Sam and Daniel already waiting. They looked incongruously aimless amongst the bustle of homegoing workers. All around were the remains of the market. Rotting vegetable peels and disintegrating cardboard boxes littered the pavements. Only the end stalls, the ones which concentrated on plastic trinkets and tinny kitchen ware, were still up. And even the few customers were finding it difficult to get attention, while around them the wares were efficiently packaged and trundled off into overnight storage. Two men, one with an uninteresting line in tea towels, the other with a display of watches up his arm were calling half-hearted attention to themselves at the same time as they kept a sharp look out for authority. It was the end of the working day, and only the street cleaners looked gloomy about it.

'Should we hide behind some bushes?' Anna said.

'Which bushes were you thinking of?' I asked. 'No green in this area, unless you're thinking of hiding under a pile of rotten cabbages. There are some iron railings on offer, but it hardly gives the same effect does it? Just fade into the distance,' I said, and then immediately took it back. 'Not too far. Stay close enough in case anybody makes a grab for me.'

We arranged ourselves in formation and stood waiting. By 6.15,

I had managed to gain only one piece of information about the saxophone snatcher. He wasn't an obsessively punctual type.

Six thirty, and the foot shuffling was growing intense. I had long got tired of staring at my watch face. What with the traffic dust settling on my face, and the number of people who tried to walk through me and over my toes, I was getting tetchy. My friends weren't bearing up much better; after another ten minutes, we decided that it was all an elaborate hoax. The waiting had calmed me down, but I was beginning to feel jumpy again. I dreaded going back to my flat. What would I find there?

We started to leave. We'd only gone a few yards when we were stopped by a loud screech. I turned to face Kingsland Road just in time to see a blue Ford drive straight into the back of a Marples lorry. At first sight it was an ordinary collision: businessman in Ford thinking about his ulcer rather than the traffic light. A few bored passers-by stuck around, but most of us had seen it all before and weren't interested. And then the driver of the lorry jumped out, white-faced, ran to the front wheel, bent down and looked intently at the ground. There was a pause before he straightened himself, gesticulating wildly.

The other driver, who'd got out of his Ford and was standing in the road, had his fist raised. For a moment the two men made together a bizarre still. Then their shouts collided, each trying to be heard above the other's indignation. The Ford man should have saved his breath. His opponent was much better at projection.

As we moved closer, his words became distinct.

'What maniac would do that,' he was shouting. 'I thought it was alive.' In his hand something bronze glittered.

'Oh no, I've got a horrible feeling that's my saxophone,' I said.

'And I've got a horrible feeling that that was your saxophone,' Anna said. 'It's been run over.'

Attracted by the unexpected drama, a crowd had formed around the two vehicles. While we waited on the sidelines, Daniel manoeuvred his way into the middle. When he came back, he was looking grim.

'That's your alto all right. The driver said somebody threw it out of a dirty white mini.'

For the second time that day, I felt like I'd had enough. Why were they doing this to me? And who were they?

'Let's go before we bump into PC Jones,' Anna said. 'He might decide to question us. I think we could all do without that.'

We left the alto where it lay. The two drivers were now into heavy mutual recrimination. Miscellaneous members of the crowd aligned themselves with one or other. The most piercing of all was the voice of an old woman, ostensibly defending the driver of the Ford, but seizing the opportunity to advocate pedestrian power.

I went back to my flat, collected a few clothes and slammed the door hastily behind me. We drove to Cardozo Road, where Sam and I picked up my car.

As usual, the anxiety had given me hunger pains. My metabolism always speeds up at the first signs of action, and I don't have that many fat reserves. We were too tired to use much imagination, so we dropped into the Essex Road Greek for a quick kebab. It wasn't a great meal, with its overdose of onions, but it warmed me up inside.

Outside, matters had also improved. The sky was almost midnight blue against the street lights, and it helped to relax people in the street. We made our way to Covent Garden, walked around star gazing, and then took in a coffee and brandy. By the time we reached Sam's flat, life seemed good again.

4.

Thursday morning wasn't so promising. Matthew's mother had obviously had enough of the slotinitis situation and dropped him round at what seemed like the crack of dawn. I tried to pretend he wasn't there and stayed in bed with my eyes firmly shut. It didn't work for long. Matthew, suffering from a surfeit of nursery care, was in one of his more rebellious moods. He flung open the bedroom door and subjected me to a long hard stare.

'Hi,' I said weakly.

'What's she doing here?' he shouted.

Sam and I exchanged an exasperated glance. It looked like my period of grace with Matthew had expired.

'She's my girlfriend,' Sam said.

'No, she's not,' the reply came quick.

'It doesn't mean I love you any the less,' Sam had been through this one many times and it came out automatically.

'She's not,' Matthew said stubbornly.

'Why not?' I asked.

'Because you're not a girl. You're big,' he said.

'Okay, then, she's my lover,'Sam offered.

'She can't be. You're not married,' Matthew said, and marched out. He came back immediately.

'A woman,' he said. 'You're his woman friend, and I'm very, very sick. Where's Batman?'

'In your room,' Sam said, and Matthew left again.

'Come on, my women friend,' Sam said. 'You've got a heavy day of detecting ahead.'

'But I don't know what to do next,' I moaned.

'Think. With your imagination, something will come.'

I thought. I thought through a curd cheese omelette I made for the three of us, through one cup of jasmine tea and another of coffee, and through an extended game of what Matthew called chasing and which seemed to consist of his jumping on me. At last something surfaced.

'What was that friend of yours called?' I asked Sam. 'The one with the languid eyes and nervous hands.'

'Tony,' he said. 'Works at *Street Times*.'

'That's the one. What's the matter with him?'

'That's what you've come up with?' Sam was incredulous.

'What? No. Could you give him a ring and ask if he knows about Tim's interest in the lonely hearts column. And ask him to send some back issues?'

'Sure. It won't be a problem. He's always eager to help. Especially women.'

'So what is the matter with him?'

'He's always eager to help but it never gets him anywhere. He wants a permanent relationship, but nothing seems to work.'

'I could tell him why,' I said.

'Yeah, I know. Its's the languid eyes and nervous hands. You better get to work. Your one-liners are becoming predictable.'

That was easier said than done. I got stuck halfway out of the door, with Matthew on the floor clasping both my feet in his grip. Only by co-ordinating a surge forwards with a sneaky tickling attack, did I manage to escape.

The Tony gambit hadn't really solved my problem of what to do next. There seemed no point in travelling all the way to Soho for a few more evasions from AER. So instead, I decided to go and pick Greta's brains. It would at least give me an opportunity to find out whether the window menders had done their work.

Greta took a long time to answer my knock. She looked dishevelled, as though she had just dragged herself from bed. She was wearing a baby-blue item, a sort of housecoat, I suppose, with its belt hugged tightly around her. She didn't seem at all pleased to see me but put up no resistance when I walked in.

We went to the kitchen, the centre of Greta's flat. It should have been an appealingly warm room with its wash of primary colours. But it always seemed to be somehow unsettled and unsettling. Perhaps because it contained no food which wasn't dried, bottled and precisely labelled. Rows of grains vied with an astonishing variety of beans to show that Greta knew her health food shops.

By the look on her face, that wasn't all that Greta knew. Her shaking hand, as she prepared an intricate mix of teas, betrayed her nervousness. I tried a few openings, but none of them got very far. Even a mention of the apprentice guitarist next door left her unmoved.

I was beginning to get irritated by the sound of my own bright chatter. I put my hand into my pockets, got out my keys and started to play with them. Greta jumped. And I twigged.

'Did you let him in?' I asked.

But Greta was prepared. 'The window mender? No he hasn't come yet.'

'I phoned him and he said he couldn't get access,' I lied.

'I was out,' she stuttered.

'It was this morning. At nine,' I said.

'I've lost the key,' she answered more slowly.

'Lost, where?'

She assumed a tone of affronted dignity.

'This is my flat,' she said. 'I like to live separately, as you well know. I only kept your key with the utmost reluctance. Now if you don't mind, I've got work to do and I'd like you out.'

'Let me put it this way.' It was my turn to speak slowly. 'If you gave my key to a man who got himself killed, or who carried dead bodies in and out, I'd like to know. Not because it might make you look foolish, but because I would go and change the lock.'

The one thing that Greta and I had in common was that we both lived, at least part of the time, alone. It was what kept us friend-ly, even when my cream intake and her grains seemed to pose enormous epistemological issues between us. Greta knew this just as well as I did. She dropped her head, so that I was gazing at the tight parting on her scalp.

'He said he was a friend of yours. And that he knew Miranda Johnson.'

'So you gave him my key?'

'Well, I was trying to meditate and couldn't be disturbed. It was bad enough answering the door. He understood and was quite nice about it.'

'I bet he was,' I said and then instantly regretted it. I tried to pass off any hint of recriminaton. 'Was there just one man?'

'Yes, and I saw him coming down with your ...' she gulped. I gritted my teeth. 'With my alto?'

'Well, how was I to know? He said he was a friend of yours.'

'Some friend,' I said.

'He seemed friendly. I even had a conversation with him about breathing techniques and wind instruments. I have a lot of ex-perience from my yoga training, and you've never been interested.'

This was too much. 'You let a stranger into my flat and then you taught him how to play my saxophone just before he went and threw it under a car?'

'How was I to know?' Her head went down again, and her voice now a low sort of whine.

'What did he look like?' I asked.

'He was dressed in blue and had a nice face, although I found it a bit uptight. Black hair. It was clean, I noticed, and well cut;

layered, like they do it these days. Blue eyes, feathery eyebrows and not many eyelashes. His mouth was tight and thin. Straight nose, bad posture. That's all I noticed.'

That was all? Greta was in the wrong profession. She should have joined one of the intelligence agencies.

'One other thing,' she said. 'He was a South African.'

I suppose I should have been grateful to her. At least she'd described the man who was lying on the floor. A man, it now appeared, who couldn't have been dead. Maybe I'd imagined him lying on the floor. Maybe, I thought, I'd better get out of there before I did any more imagining.

I left her sitting, her head still bowed. Her voice followed me out, a pleading tone in it.

'If you want help changing the lock, Kate, come and get me.'

'Thanks,' I called. For nothing, I thought.

I bought a lock and spent the next hour venting my rage on fitting it. The job I did was adequate if untidy, which is more than I could say for my damaged room. I decided it was morbid to stick around too long, so I banged the door with a flourish and made my way to Miranda Johnson's.

She lived a few blocks away in a house which had withstood the ravages of time, so far. The last few years had seen a transformation in the surrounding property. Doors and windows were painted a variety of murky, if elegant, shades of browns and greens. Front gardens were neatly planned and promptly weeded. Not so number 86. It stood out defiantly; its colour scheme a rampant mix of blues and purples. For all I knew, its front garden could have been weed free, but it was difficult to tell beneath the towering grass.

By the side of the door was a succession of bell pushes. I tried them all, but hearing no sound I applied myself to the brass knocker. I was on the second swing when the door opened, and my momentum carried me into Miranda. We disengaged ourselves.

'Green,' I said.

Miranda stopped squinting at the bright sunlight and threw me a vague smile.

'What? Oh, my hair. Yes, I got bored with the pink. Come in Kate. I was just thinking of you.'

She led me throgh an obstacle course of three bicycles, one pram and battered-looking typewriter, into her study. It was one of the few genuinely eclectic rooms I've ever come across. A mass of different styles clashed and merged. Her desk occupied one wall, and it bore the stamp of Miranda's prodigious productions. Opposite, a lone harp stood, its strings atangle. In between, was a pile of cushions ranging from 1950s dingy to Habitat modern, a keelam which would have looked fine if it wasn't surrounded by rush matting of dubious origins, and what seemed to be a porcelain bath tub. The walls were white, newly painted and bare. I was still accommodating the sensory impact when Miranda spoke.

'What are you?' she said.

'What am I ?' It came out with what my school drama teacher had liked to call a rising intonation.

'Your star sign.'

'Pisces.'

'Ever had your chart read? Would you like some tea?'

'No, I haven't. And no thanks, I've just had some.'

'I do,' she said. 'Back in a minute.'

I moved to her desk and glanced at the work in progress. Miranda cultivated an air of eccentricity which had deceived many a colleague. She was a skilled academic who knew how to play the system and how to fool it. She was in her late forties, had been a standard bearer of student rebellion in 1968 and had gone on to become a media star, interviewed whenever students tried anything radical. She'd avoided being branded a sell-out because of her open contempt for authority, her constant changes in focus and her eccentric fashion sense with her constantly changing hair colour. The latest in a long line of changes was her recent attachment to astrology. No one understood why. I suspected her of being more than a little tongue-in-cheek about it. Years of committee life had made Miranda devious. Talking about star signs seemed like another ploy on her part to pass judgements while staying impartial.

She came back, balancing an oversized French coffee cup, and sat on the cushion arrangement. I chose the side of the bath, after gazing at the enormous fish inside it.

'I'm looking for a man,' I said. 'Greta said you knew him.' I related Greta's description.

'What colour did you say his eyes were?' she said.

'Greta remembers them as blue.'

'Greta is always right about details. I don't suppose you have any idea what his sun sign was,' she said.

'No, I don't.'

'Too bad,' she said. 'I never forget a chart.'

She lapsed into intense concentration; one hand absentmindedly twiddling with her green hair. It seemed like a long time before she spoke again.

'Sounds like a man who came to my evening class.'

'Which one? Do you mean Astral Projection and ...' my voice floundered.

'And Revolutionary Marxism, APARM for short. Good name, isn't it? I didn't want the usual students, so I designed a course with an new approach. Worked to some extent.'

'Oh, good. Now about the man?'

'Came to my course. I read all my students' charts, and he sounds like the Gemini with Capricorn rising and Mars in Pisces. That won't help much, will it?'

'I'm not sure. What does it mean?'

She put her tea down and eased backwards.

'Gemini is a mutable sign,' she said. 'Geminis tend to see things in terms of ideas and are very interested in what other people think of them. They weigh everything up on a rational level and as a result they have trouble with decisions because they don't consider the emotional issues. Pose themselves false questions.'

'And what about the Mars in Pisces bit?'

'Can be difficult. Fire hitting water. Mars is about doing what you want, while Pisces are very sensitive to the needs of others.'

'That sounds like a clash.'

'Exactly. Now the Capricorn rising is a different aspect Capricorn's an earth sign — makes for serious, good organisers. If it's rising, that means the sun's below the horizon, which would make the person, not introverted, rather more self-concerned. World can be frightening for Capricorns. They need a lot of security.'

'And what happens if they don't get it?' I asked. Being knocked out in strange flats wouldn't make anybody feel too safe.

Miranda frowned. 'I can only give you my interpretation,' she said. 'Other people may say slightly different things, although, in principle, I think we'd all agree. At a guess, an insecure Gemini with Capricorn rising could become paranoid. His head would try and rationalise why he's alone, and he would be pulled between feeling persecuted and being very self-judging.'

'Sounds like a mess,' I said.

'Could say that,' she said. 'I'm not into judgements.'

'Are you sure you can't remember his name? Don't you keep a register of students?'

'Given it up,' she said. 'Provides an excuse for colleges to close courses, if not enough attend.'

'How do people know about the course? Do you advertise?'

'Different ways. Mostly word of mouth. Let me try and think how David heard about it.'

'Did you say David?' I snapped.

'That's right, now you come to mention it, his name was David. Funny that, things you forget always come out when you stop concentrating. Never knew his surname. Came to me through a complicated network. Knew somebody in the States who was a friend of the sister of one of the women in my old women's group.'

'So, you don't know anybody who knew him first hand?'

'Afraid not. You know how involved things get. David was more shadowy than most. Always charming, but couldn't get much out of him.'

'It's very important that I find this David. Is there anything else you know that might lead me to him?'

A furrow settled between her neatly plucked eyebrows.

'One clue,' she said. 'He was met after class by a woman. Strange American accent with a smart car. Remember her because we talked about the Covent Garden sauna.'

'The Paradise?' I asked.

'Yes. She went there. I was saying how coarse the cold makes my skin, and she suggested I try it. Perhaps you could find her there.'

'You didn't catch her name?'

'Never knew it. Did feel her skin and it was smooth. Was about forty, looked healthy. Sort of vivid brown-red hair. Henna, I guessed. My length, but straighter. Short, quite well built, but wearing a fur coat, so that could have been deceptive. Loud voice, seemed jumpy. Not very tall — wears high heels — probably about five foot three.'

Miranda pulled herself up and went to her desk, signalling the end of the interview.

'I'd better go,' I said. 'Thanks for your help. I'll drop by sometime and get my chart read.'

She was sorting through some papers and didn't turn round. I shrugged and walked out.

'Don't seem able to find it,' she called.

'Find what?' I stopped.

'Article I thought you'd be interested in. That's why I was thinking about you when you came. Must have been psychic.'

'Oh, the article,' I said. 'Never mind. You can always drop it in when you pass by the house. Bye now.'

I got back to Sam's flat to find a note waiting for me. 'Gone to catch some natural history,' it read. 'Tony says he'll investigate. Phone Daniel and Ron.' I dialled the Cardozo Road number. Daniel answered on the second ring.

'I bet you didn't know that the Davey Safety Lamp made life unsafe for miners,' he said.

'You been meddling with the books in the BM again?' I asked.

'Where else? Although I did hit the public records library the other day, and they had some great stuff on the Chartist riots. But I didn't ring to tell you that. Today at the BM I sat next to Karen Frazer, you know the Soviet historian who produces a range of scholastic books with twelve footnotes per paragraph and a bibliography that adds a new dimension to reading. How does she do it?'

'Don't you start,' I said. I've had about all I can take from Greta. I'm sure she's getting worse. You know the other day I bumped into her leaving the house in her slippers. I thought she might have forgotten her shoes, but no. I was forced to listen to a long and very boring explanation of precisely why her slippers were necessary.'

'And why were they?' Daniel asked.

'Couldn't work it out. My theory is that she really had forgotten to put her shoes on, but she was too embarrassed to say so. Anyway, today I discovered that she let the murdered man into the flat. He said he was a friend of Miranda Johnson — Greta reckons that any friend of Miranda should have free access to my flat.'

'So, did Miranda know him?'

'No, he was an ex-student of hers. Went to her APARM course.'

'APARM?'

'Don't worry about it. She's dyed her hair green and completely given up using pronouns to start sentences.'

'Karen Frazer could supply her with some. I got talking to her in the coffee queue at the BM, which is why I phoned you. She said she knew Tim Nicholson and that before his death he asked her a lot of questions about Czarist intelligence services and infiltration of the Bolsheviks before the revolution. He asked her if she thought she would ever be deceived by a spy.'

'And what did she say?'

'She didn't relate to it at the time. She's the type who's sensitive enough to wonder what he was really getting at, but not interested enough to find out. It's the English intellectual approach to life, where somebody else's problems are dangerous territory. But I think you should take it seriously. Maybe you should find out why Tim was interested in spies.'

We were in the middle of a complicated speculation when the doorbell rang. I said goodbye to Daniel and went to answer it.

'Hi, Ron,' I said. 'I was just about to ring you.'

'I'd like to talk to you. In confidence,' he said.

I beckoned him in to a seat. He refused an offer of coffee and started before I had time to sit down. His delicate white hands worried at his sandy moustache.

'This is not easy for me. But I think you ought to know,' he said.

I nodded non-commitally.

'It's about Friday evening. Michael wasn't the only one who went back to the office. Somebody else did.'

'Such as who?'

There was no reply.

'Was it you?'

He shook his head.

'Then was it Aldwyn?'

'I don't like doing this,' he said. 'Aldwyn couldn't kill anyone. But I think you ought to know, because he might be able to tell you something. Just after we got to the pub, we started a conversation about … about AER. Aldwyn said he'd go back and see Tim.'

'What time was this?' I asked.

'Six-thirty. He was only gone for twenty minutes, and the pub's quite a walk away, so he couldn't have been there long.'

'Did he tell you what happened?'

'No … he didn't say much.'

'So, what were you talking about that made Aldwyn go back?'

'Just routine business,' he muttered.

'Like spying?'

He tried to deny it, but he wasn't very convincing. I repeated the question.

'Tim was weird. I mean he was acting weird for a few weeks before he … fell. It was like he didn't trust us. First he got excited about his work on the Argentina connection and then he clammed up. It was creating a lot of tension, and Aldwyn decided to have it out with him,' he said.

'So, what happened? Are you sure Aldwyn wasn't gone long?'

'Of course, I'm sure,' he snapped. 'I met a friend and we got to talking about models. We were only just getting into it, when Aldwyn returned.'

'Models? Things are getting bad.'

Ron threw me an exasperated look. 'Model ships,' he said, 'are my hobby. And now I'm going home. I haven't been sleeping well. I'm taking the afternoon off.'

With that he left. For the second time that day, I toyed with the idea of going to the Carelton Building. Once again I decided against it. Instead, I dialled the number of AER. A harassed Aldwyn answered.

'Please don't be long, Kate,' he said. 'I'm alone in the office, and there is a tremendous amount to do.'

'I'll get to the point then,' I said. 'Why didn't you tell me you went to see Tim on Friday?'

ed gasp, but it could have been my
i...

... said. 'I wouldn't care to think that
p... on my part, would interfere in this
in... eel that I should say … well let me
pu... ver liked Tim Nicholson.' He threw
th... ight backfire on him.

... omething more original. The fact
tha... got on wasn't news to me. I would
hav... wyn had told me whom he actually
lik...

A... understanding. He carried on.
'I... se I have no right to say this. But
I co... u to keep it completely confiden-
tial.

'I... ck to the office to tell Tim you
didn...

'Pl... ivolous. I went back to the office
to cle... been worrying me.'

'An... you. I asked. 'Clear it up, I mean?'

'As a matter of fact, I was unable to. Tim was talking to a woman
friend, and I decided it was not the time to do our dirty washing.'

'What exactly was the nature of this washing?' I said.

'Tim had made certain insinuations of a private nature. I don't
consider that they are your concern. Now if that is all?'

'Just a minute, Aldwyn,' I said. 'Let me get this right. First
you withhold information, you keep silent about your visit to Tim.
And now you won't tell me why you went back.'

'I wouldn't have put it in quite such a conspiratorial manner.
But if that's how you want to treat my professional caution, that
is your affair,' he said.

I tried another tack.

'Tell me about spies?' I said. 'I gather Tim was interested in
them.'

'Who told you that?' he said. He sounded anxious.

'Sorry,' I said. 'Professional caution and all that. Was that why
you went to see Tim?'

Aldwyn's voice sounded like it was coming from far away. I

could picture him, sitting alone in that crowded office, holding the receiver as if it was contaminated.

'I don't like to do this. But since you have obviously delved in these murky waters, I had better set the record straight. Tim was, in my opinion, unbalanced. He had fantasies. He insisted that our organisation had been infiltrated. Of course, this was utter nonsense, and I felt it my duty to inform him accordingly. As it happened, I didn't have the chance. Now, that is academic.'

'I wonder,' I said. 'Why don't you expand on the fantasies?'

'I will not. This is as far as I am willing to commit myself. We cannot afford to be slap happy about the information, especially unreliable information, that comes our way.'

'Don't I know it,' I said. 'You never can tell who you can trust. Did you recognise the woman Tim was talking to?'

'I had never seen her before, Tim did not introduce us. Despite his background, Tim didn't have many social graces. I left because I felt I was interfering in their private affairs.'

'What was the atmosphere like?' I said.

'I did not dwell on it. Neither of them seemed very happy, but I dismissed this from my mind. As you know I never ...'

'... really liked Tim,' I said. 'Well, if you see the woman again, tell me, please. Maybe she'll be at the funeral tomorrow.'

'Perhaps,' he said. 'And I must go now. I'm rather pleased I decided to tell you about my visit. It clears my conscience.'

As I put the phone down, Matthew came bounding into the room. He thrust a picture at me.

'Just what I was waiting for,' I said. 'A stegasorous.'

Matthew grabbed it away. 'It's not, it's a dinosaur.'

I pointed to the caption. 'Well, it says stegasorous.'

Matthew thought for a while and then threw himself righteously into the battle.

'It's a stebasorous, STEBASOROUS not ... not ... what you said,' he shouted.

I resorted to my ultimate tactic. 'Look, you four-and-a-half-year-old. Which one of us can read?'

Usually this would work, but Matthew is a constant innovator and he found a way out of it.

'Me and you,' he said proudly, and grabbed a pen with which

he wrote an imitation of his name along my arm.

I was still trying to wash it off when Sam walked in wearily. He plonked himself down into an armchair while Matthew got stuck into play school. I went into the bedroom and searched vainly for a book I hadn't read. I gave up and ran a bath instead. Just as I was soaking myself loose, Sam came in.

'I'm exhausted,' he said. 'The Natural History Museum's a zoo. Oh, I forgot to tell you, Maria phoned and invited you over. Her household is having some sort of celebration tonight.'

I arrived at the huge house in Highgate Crescent and looked at it, impressed. Maria and her friends had been squatting for years in North London and had got used to the constant moves from house to house. I rang the bell and waited while somebody, ever security conscious, inspected me from an upstairs window. The house, with its large bay windows, sat on a hill overlooking Highgate woods. Not a bad location at all, and I'd heard rumours that they'd been licensed by the council and might be there to stay.

The door swung open. I faced a palatial if crumbling entrance hall and a tall man who smilingly gestured at me. I started to return the smile and then I looked again. The man had no features. I was looking at a face which was white, pure unadulterated white. Only a pair of weak brown eyes and vaguely pink mouth interrupted the severity of it all.

'Is Maria in?' I asked nervously.

He pushed one leg out to prevent a noisy three-year-old from escaping out of the door. 'She is, come,' he said.

I stepped inside and looked around me, wondering which door to try. The man, with the child now safely perched on his shoulders, gestured me to the stairs and into the basement.

The kitchen was packed with an assortment of people all busily cooking, stirring and talking. I was relieved when I spotted Maria in the corner, cutting fruit into a punch. Only when I was sitting beside her did I feel relaxed enough to take in my surroundings.

It was a large room, but it looked as though, without the mass of people, it could be cosy. Maria's household always made sure that at least they ate in comfortable surroundings. True, the decoration was pure cover-up − it wasn't worth doing much basic work, given the constant moves − but a lot of imagination had gone into

55

it. Imagination wasn't lacking among the people either. A good half of them were in fancy dress, and several had painted their faces white. Three children, perched on a corner window seat, were intent on covering their faces in lurid colours.

'Is this a normal party or have I bust in on something special?' I asked the woman next to me tentatively. Her clothes, baggy around her, gave her the look of a neglected child, and the permanent smile she wore on her face didn't look quite true.

'It's special,' she answered cheerfully. 'We're celebrating birthdays.'

'Whose?' I said.

She stopped cutting cabbage and held her knife in mid-air. She looked at me doubtfully.

'What do you mean ...?' She started to say before comprehension dawned.

'Oh, I get you. It's not like that. We're holding a cosmic birthday, a communal exploration of all our lives. We're so busy most of the time, you see, if we celebrate one mass birthday, it saves us organising individually. You can't be too rigid about these things, can you?'

I gulped and turned to Maria, who had been listening to the exchange with a broad smile on her face. She was always amused at my attempts to merge into her lifestyle. We both knew how different mine really was. She finished with the punch, poured us each a glass and then showed me round the house.

The tour ended in the sitting-room. Again on a vast scale, its glass doors opened onto a promising garden. The kitchen contingent had drifted in, and the air was thick with smoke. Maria and I selected some of the big cushions that stood in for furniture, and we settled against the wall. Within minutes, one of the painted children delivered our food. We ate the bright, if indistinguished combination and chatted politely. But things livened up after people finished with their plates and got to the joints. Maria and I swapped selected highlights from our lives. I'd known her since I first arrived in England, and no matter how infrequently we met, we always found it easy to talk to each other.

So there I was, oversweet trifle by my side and a glass of wine in my hand, describing the mechanics of the detective business.

With distance, the story was entertaining, so I wasn't particularly surprised when I noticed that the man seated next to Maria was openly listening. His features were blotted out by a massive dose of white paint.

It was all right to begin with, mostly I just avoided his gaze. But after a while I started to feel uncomfortable. The man wasn't just listening casually; he was staring at me intently. It was too aggressive. I faltered. Maria turned to see what was putting me off, but she found nothing particularly odd. I told myself that I was being paranoid, that probably he was too stoned to move his gaze. I forced myself to carry on.

I didn't get far. Abruptly the man craned his neck until his face almost touched Maria's. She threw me a puzzled look, but didn't know how to react. He was too close for focus so I leaned away.

It was a shock. I thought there was something familiar about him. Suddenly it clicked into place. He was the dead man, the man who'd been lying in my flat. In speechless fright, I gripped Maria's hand. She squeezed back reassuringly.

I forced myself to speak.

'What were you doing in my flat?' I asked.

At first the man didn't reply: he just stared. Then, in a stoned stage whisper, he said, 'Stop investigating,' before leaping up and walking quickly through the French doors that lead to the garden.

I watched him go without moving a muscle. Only when he'd disappeared was I able to think properly. I stood up, yanking Maria onto her feet, and dragged her with me towards the garden.

'It's him,' I shouted.

'Who?' Maria said, trying half-heartedly to resist.

'The man in my flat. Don't leave me, I think he's mad.'

As soon as she'd got the picture, Maria was willing to move. Together, we rushed down the overgrown garden towards the back wall. But we'd started too late. By the time we'd reached it, the man was nowhere in sight. I stubbed my toe on a small heap of bricks and, swearing loudly, balanced on them to look over the wall. A surrealist sight greeted me. It was one of those redevelopment plots which had run out of money, and the half-bulldozed houses looked like council follies. Bricks, weeds and bureaucracy competed with the local people who were trying to build a communal-cum-children's garden in its place. As evidence of this scheme, a few mangy peacocks were picking apathetically in the dirt.

Maria and I pushed each other over the wall and straight into some brambles. It was the last straw. By the time we'd managed to disentangle and comfort each other, there didn't seem much point in further pursuit. Dispirited, we returned to the other side.

Back in the garden, two people who'd been jolted out of their living-room stupor by our shouts, stared. 'Far out,' they both said simultaneously, before wandering off. Rubbing our reddened legs, we walked back to the house.

Inside, a pall of smoke hung, making fresh air nothing but a pleasant memory. I was exhausted. Leaning against the wall, I slid down until I was seated, head back. For a while, I closed my eyes, as the conversation from different parts of the room mixed into a weird jumble. If I'd been on the ball, I could have learnt about the latest microprocessor, the inner dynamics of being an exploited baker, or the recipe for the newest cocktail. But all I could do was get back my breath and wait until I felt safe enough to open my eyes.

Maria had never seen the man before.

'You get all types here,' she said.

'So I see.'

I began working round the circle of people; asking for some kind of positive identification. It was hard work. I could understand their resistance. Everybody was trying to relax and have a good time, and I was worrying at them — trying to focus when they were into expansion. But I persisted, and after a while the inquiry caught on like a fashion. Halfway round the circle, people started to concentrate, in that stoned sort of way. The conversation became a game.

'Never even saw him,' somebody said. 'Was he pretty?'

'Couldn't really tell. You know, I'm not sure I like all this white paint. I think it's a bit severe, suppresses the natural features,' said a man who had gone against the trend and painted his face red and green. He looked sick, but it might have been because his decor clashed with his yellow tunic and orange tights.

'He stole my biscuit,' said a six-year-old, who'd earlier

adamantly refused to go to bed and was now using every tactic to get into the conversation.

'Maybe he's one of those nuts from the primal therapy house. They're heavily into screaming, so he probably thinks he's doing Kate good by scaring her,' a drunken wit slurred.

His contribution widened the fantasy stakes. Soon they were all trying to outdo each other in providing bizarre explanations. I could only take so much. I sat back and concentrated on the sound of B B King weaving through the talk.

Gradually a side argument reached me.

A woman was irritated. 'Nick? That's just ridiculous. You can't say that. I mean, how many Nicks do we each know? There's a Nick lives here, Nick next door, the milkman's name is Nick ...'

Beside her, another woman was feebly trying to interrupt this flow of indignation.

'Did you really mean Nick?' I asked.

She looked at me and frowned.

'There's even two Nicks in this room at this very moment,' her neighbour continued. Meanwhile, the woman was searching her memory.

'No. It's Nicher, Nicotine — that's it, Nicholas. No, no that's not right, wait a minute.'

'Let's face it, Nick is an overused name.'

'Nicholson,' I said.

She gave a beautiful smile. 'That's it, Nicholson. What a relief, thanks a lot. You know how it is: you forget a name and then become obsessed by it.'

Heart thumping, I waited for more.

'What about it?' I asked after we'd faced each other for a decent interval.

'What?' she said blankly.

'What about Nicholson? Did you mean Tim Nicholson?'

'Yes,' she said. 'I knew him. He's dead. Didn't you hear about it?'

'Yeah, I heard. So what about him?' I said through clenched teeth.

She looked at me like I was crazy. 'Oh ... I was just saying that I've seen that man — the one you were asking about — with

Tim Nicholson.'

'Where did you see them?' I asked, excited.

'At Camden Lock about two weeks ago. They were having some sort of argument and they both looked angry. So I said a brief hello and left them to it. I invited Tim here and then thought that was rude. So I invited the other man as well. Gave him the address.'

'Did you catch his name?' I asked.

'David something,' she said, the interest leaving her voice. 'I'm not into surnames.'

After that, the conversation veered away. I sat for a while and then, making my goodbyes to Maria, I left.

'She stole my biscuit,' the voice of the six-year-old accused.

Sam was sitting up in bed scribbling when I got back. He threw me an absentminded greeting.

'What's the matter?' I said.

'I'm stuck on the last line. I'm trying to find a word to describe an image of two old people digging in a river for gold.'

'Try panning,' I said, and then, when he shook his head, I pulled more words out, staccato fashion, 'Searching, rolling, scrabbling, looking, fiddling, fighting, scrambling ...'

Sam looked up in amusement. 'Okay, Kate, talking to you about poetry is like talking to Matthew about chateau wines. What happened to you to make you so speedy?'

I told him, taking him through the whole day. When I finished, Sam looked confused.

'Shit, your story's as bad as QCD,' he said.

'What are you on about?' I asked, annoyed.

'It's not me, it's that student. He phoned again and I had to tell him Matthew was having hysterics before he got off. He's got his teeth into QCD — quantum chromo dynamics — and he keeps bugging me about it. Frankly, I don't know what he's talking about half the time and I keep telling him it's not my subject. But he thinks I'm the teacher and ought to know everything.'

Sam's voice tailed off at the end of the speech and, muttering about how tired he was, he turned over, ready for sleep. I undressed and got into bed, trying a few opening gambits to raise Sam's interest. Eventually, I prodded his back.

'You know,' I said, 'I was thinking about you today and trying to think of a man I'd rather be with.'

That got him. 'And who did you come up with?' he asked quickly.

'I discovered I don't have many men friends.'

Sam laughed. He moved close until his back nestled into my body. I gave up on the words and went with the contact. We made love, and only when we were both drifting into sleep, did I make another half-hearted attempt to get him to interpret my evening. It didn't work.

5.

Friday morning showed a clear blue sky. I woke with a smile on my face, and I'd just turned to share it with Sam when the inevitable happened. The phone rang. Sam and I slipped into our usual routine. He wrestled with my compulsion to answer, while I tried to explain why it was that I couldn't ignore phones.

Sam didn't go for any argument that my association of phones with disaster was an early childhood phobia that it would be risky to resist. But he didn't stop me when I picked it up. He got his victory, though, when I made a face at the voice. It was the fussy editor of a struggling magazine who occasionally dropped work my way and then chased me for it ever after. This time he wanted me and my friend Lowri to check the alterations that he'd made to our article on the London jazz scene. I knew there'd be nothing wrong with his edit — there never was — but he wouldn't be convinced. In the end I had to agree, because it was the only way I could get him off the phone. After that, I went through a whole performance to get hold of Lowri, who seemed to have about five phone numbers and wasn't at any of them. By the time I'd done that, I was fully awake and had lost the smile completely. I tolerated a few of Sam's teases and then we both got up; he to tend to Matthew, and I to dress. I made my way to the crematorium.

The funeral was a dreary affair. Probably for the first time, the two sides of Tim's life had come together. They didn't match, and the participants in each didn't mix. Tim's friends had commandeered the back of the hall. A few greetings were exchanged for the most part, though, people's eyes stayed fixed on the floor, the walls, their hands, anywhere but on the coffin.

The front rows contained family. This religious service was more suited to their style of life, and yet they, too, looked uncomfortable. Tim's mother, in her black mink was readily identifiable. The resemblance between her and her son was strong; but where Tim's face had combined cynicism with hope, hers was set in a mould of bitter disappointment. She was surrounded by women and men of indefinite ages but definite wealth. Around them slumped younger members of the family, their poses ranging from the bored to the frankly asleep. I caught Aldwyn's eye and nodded in their direction. He shook his head. The woman he'd seen with Tim wasn't there.

I recognised one other person. Robert Slick was sitting isolated in the third row. I wondered whether it was usual for lawyers to attend the funerals of their clients.

The priest was embarrassed. He'd obviously never met Tim, and he went on too long in compensation. When the coffin finally coasted to its mysterious destination behind the tacky black curtain, I shed a few tears, as did some others of Tim's friends. His family remained dry eyed. The whole performance had taken fifteen minutes. We shuffled out of one door as the next mourning party waited at another.

Groups of people hung around outside as if unsure of the correct etiquette. Mrs Nicholson stood to one side. Surrounded by murmuring well-wishers, she held her head erect with disdain. Two strands of pearls accentuated the length of her neck and confirmed my guess that her simple black dress had been acquired at a not so simple price.

'Coming for a drink?' Ron whispered in my ear. 'We're going to try talking about Tim without the bullshit ceremony.'

'I'd like to,' I said. 'But I think I'd better talk to Tim's mother.'

'Good luck to you. I've already tried. She gave me such a look, I backed away immediately.'

I left him and walked towards Mrs Nicholson. Two women, their diamond rings flashing in the sunlight, their sternly styled skirts and blouses giving a simultaneous impression of dowdiness and wealth, stood at a distance from her. I passed them on my way.

'A damned cheek,' one said in her loud, round tones. 'He should have displayed some signs of decency on an occasion such as this. I honestly can't say ...'

'But, darling,' the other one interrupted. 'We shouldn't be malicious. After all, if what was said was true, can we really blame the man? And it is over twenty-five years ago, after all.'

'That doesn't excuse his behaviour. Don't you recall the manner in which he threw her over when Malcolm became so dramatic. If you ask me, there is absolutely no good in the man ... And talking about no good, did you see those persons at the back? Fortunately, they kept well away ...'

I had reached Tim's mother. I introduced myself and held out my hand. She gave me hers. It was unringed and lifeless. It lay in mine for a cold, dry second and then slipped out again.

'Could you spare me a minute?' I said. 'I'm a friend of Tim's and I'd like to ask you a few questions.'

Her calculating eyes looked down her aquiline nose. Her mouth made a tight line and stayed that way.

'I really don't consider this the time, do you, dear?' her voice rang out. The tone was so hostile, I understood why Ron had backed off so quickly.

'It's important,' I said. 'I'm investigating Tim's death and there might be a lead you could give me.'

'I cannot help you. I have had very little contact with my son in the last five years. Besides, I gather the police are satisfied that he fell.' She turned to go, but found herself facing Robert Slick. She did a complete circle until she was facing me again.

'Elizabeth,' Slick's voice came from behind her. 'Surely we should talk.'

'I'm sorry, Robert, the time for that has passed. I am, as you can see, talking to this young lady. So if you wouldn't mind ...' she had gripped my elbow and I found myself being propelled along a gravel path and into the gardens.

'You don't like Robert Slick?' I asked.

63

'Dreadful little man. I can't think what on earth possessed me to ...' she stopped and regarded me. 'But that has absolutely nothing to do with you. What would you like to know?'

'I'm interested in locating Tim's wife,' I said.

'Are you?' She drawled, but behind the casual tones I thought I detected a strong note of hostility. 'Why?'

'I want to find out where Tim's money goes,' I said.

She threw her head back so that I saw the full sweep of her white neck and gave a laugh. There was no amusement in it.

'You're wasting your time on me. My ex-husband, Malcolm, made damn certain that I would not benefit from his money. Why don't you go and look her up in the telephone directory?'

'I tried,' I said. 'At the last count there were 530 Nicholsons in the London phone book. I don't even know her first name, whether she lives in London or even if she's kept Tim's surname.'

'If that's the extent of your investigative skills, I will not wait with bated breath for the results of your enquiry,' she threw out. 'Life is short, after all.'

It irritated me. The funeral had been enough to irritate anyone, and her behaviour wasn't helping. I decided two could play at that game.

'Why were you cut out of your husband's will?' I asked. 'And why haven't you seen Tim for so long?'

I might as well have kept my mouth shut. The only indication that the question had even penetrated was a slight tug on the gold bracelet that held her watch to her smooth white wrist. She turned to go.

'What happens if there's no will?' I asked.

She faced me once more. Her smile was triumphant. 'Now I understand,' she said. 'That is why Robert had the nerve to approach me. And for a moment I thought he was growing sentimental.'

'But he isn't?'

'Not if the will is lost. I expect that Robert's main fear is a revival of that dreary old scandal. As if anybody cares: I certainly don't.' I noticed a thin film of sweat on her forehead, which conflicted with her stylish presentation and betrayed her defiant statement. Either that, or the mink was getting to her in the warm sun. She

64

drew it tightly around her, but before she turned to go, she shot me one more calculating glance and spoke.

'Diana has not changed her surname. She's ex-directory. She lives in North London,' she rattled off an address. 'Now, I do have a long drive to Devon, so if you'll be so kind as to excuse me ...'

She turned on her heels and clicked her way decisively back along the path and out of sight.

6.

The Paradise sauna boasts of its exclusiveness. It also charges accordingly. Set in a small cobbled back street, it has a discreet plant-lined entrance hall that leads into a glass-roofed imitation jungle. The sauna, the proclaimed source of smooth skin, is situated in one corner of the enormous main room. For the rest, there's an oval green bathing area which is connected to the sauna through long, plant-lined avenues. All roads lead to the salad bar, which serves a variety of health foods at unhealthy prices. The place is designed as a luxury retreat for the modern working girl. It has all the requisite trimmings and attention to detail. Only the occasional peel of paint on the wall hints that economic troubles are getting to even the best of us.

I stood in front of the desk, eyeing the prices. The receptionist, wearing a pale-green tracksuit with 'Paradise' embossed stylishly in gold on one sleeve, looked like she'd been diligently taking the treatment. Her skin was a gloss finish; her hair done into one of those casual styles that take hours to effect, her body, taut and subtle; her face, a bland expanse. I decided against trying to get any information out of her, she looked too hostile, and instead booked myself for a full-length massage. If nothing else, I could spend the time inside working out how to deduct the treatment from my tax.

I took my towel quota — two large green and one small blue — and moved through the white slatted double doors to the changing

65

area. Screened off from the rest of the outfit by a shaky partition, it was purely functional; such facilities were clearly not part of the grand design that informed the rest of the building. A set of gray lockers faced blank walls, while a crowd of women struggled to change in and out of their expensive clothes. On one side, a queue edged slowly towards the few hair-dryers, and I gazed in astonishment at one woman intent on drying each strand individually.

I squeezed my way through the mass of bodies, many of them tanned by the southern sun or the bottle, and all of them well cared for. Eventually, after an adept bit of queue-jumping, I managed to find a locker where I undressed and stored my clothes. Then I made it out of the enclosure.

My guide — Joanne, if her diamanté nameplate was to be believed — was waiting for me just past the doorway. She gave a perfunctory smile and took me through her paces. She was either bored or hungry. Certainly she didn't have the confidence that the receptionist had on display. I waited for her to finish.

It didn't take long. She turned to go. 'If you want anything, just ask,' she said.

'There is one thing,' I said.

She turned, with an exasperated expression on her otherwise friendly face.

'What's the matter?' I asked. 'Have they put somebody on reception to time you?'

She grinned. 'Something like that. Sorry, it's been a hell of a morning, and I can't take much more. What is it you want to know?'

'I just wondered whether you usually see the same faces around here.'

'Sure, we have our regular customers. Some of our girls come in five times a week to keep their bodies in trim,' she said.

'I'm looking for a woman who comes here,' I began.

'Well, ask at the desk,' she said.

'That's the trouble, I don't know her name.'

I'd lost her sympathy. A question was one thing; an extended inquiry, another. I thought quickly.

'It's quite a problem because I've never even seen this woman.

But a friend of mine was in here once and talked to her. The thing is, I'm very close to this friend, and her birthday's due soon. She's the type who buys herself everything as soon as she spots it, so it's hard to find her presents. But she did happen to mention that this women told her about a completely new ... a new diary system — not blue star or filofax, but a whole new concept, and my friend is a stationery freak. So I want to find the woman to see if I can get hold of one of them.'

Myself, I thought the story a mite weak, but by the look of Joanne's face, it had struck home.

'Did your friend describe her?' she asked.

I breathed a sigh of relief. 'I did manage to worm some sort of description out of her, even though I didn't want to appear too interested. The woman has a light accent. About forty, and a few inches smaller than me. Red-brown hair and she wears furs — obviously wealthy. My friend says she's quite assertive.'

Joanne thought. 'Sounds like one of our regulars. A Mrs Schoenberg. That's her, over there.' She pointed in the distance to where a lone woman, dressed in white, cotton wool covering her eyes, was lying.

'Thanks a lot, Joanne,' I said.

'My name's Marylin. It was the only badge they had.'

I walked over to the woman and selected a lounger next to her. I laid myself out. She didn't make any sign that she knew or cared that I was there.

'Mrs Schoenberg?' I said, tentatively.

She removed her eyepatches and looked at me. I looked back. Miranda's description was accurate, but it had left out the air of petulance that pervaded Mrs Schoenberg's face. She must have been at least forty. She looked as though she she didn't like not getting what she wanted. It was a pity. Her sour expression spoiled the clear reddish glow of her skin, it tugged her full mouth downwards and it diminished the light in her large brown eyes.

'I don't know you,' she said. The accent was Latin American — Argentinian, I guessed, overlayed by New York. That, along with the diamond in each ear, placed her. She'd grown up in one of those middle-class Argentinian families who play polo with the junta while making sure that their children leave the country to be educated.

'My name's Kate Baeier,' I said.

'Good for you,' she said. 'And goodbye. What is it with you English? Either you don't speak at all or you approach a perfect stranger who obviously wants to be alone.'

'I'm Portuguese,' I said.

That earned me another glance. Brief interest revived in her face. It didn't last long. Just as I had guessed her background by her looks, she guessed mine. She didn't like it. She lay back again and stared at the glass roof.

I sat beside her, wondering how to continue. At last I decided that there was no crawling round the point.

'I'm looking for David,' I said.

'Go look then,' she said.

'Do you know where I could start?' I asked.

'Why should I tell you if I did?' she said. 'Leave me alone, all of you.'

'I'm worried about him,' I said. 'He looked a little white when I last saw him.'

'I couldn't care less,' she said, and her voice was bitter with anger. I decided to try playing with it.

'You too?' I asked.

'What's that supposed to mean?'

'David's been giving me the runaround. He ditched me at a party recently. I thought maybe he'd done the same to you.'

'You think you've got problems,' she shouted as she threw her hands, palms upwards, into the air. 'You feel sorry for yourself? You think he treated you badly? Well, you should know what he did to me, what I had to put up with, what he subjected me to. After all I did for him. I, Tina Schoenberg, was not raised to be treated like that. There's no respect in this country. That is why I am sick, why I have red-outs.'

I didn't comment. A black-out, okay, but a red-out? But Tina didn't need encouragement. For the next five minutes I listened to her detailed critique of life in Britain, ranging from the telephone and transport services to the general state of food. I can't say that I didn't sympathise with her, although when she concluded with the conviction that she'd caught bilharzia from the Regents park

Canal, she lost me.

'I've got a solution,' I said. 'Why don't you go and consult Marty Succulent? I'm sure he'll do wonders for your red-outs.'

'Who's he? she asked. 'Sounds like a quack.'

'Far from it. He's my osteopath and a trained acupuncturist. He's done wonders for me. I was in agony before I met him. Of course, your case is more complicated,' I put in hurriedly before she could launch into a new tirade.'But honestly, he can raise the practically dead, I swear it.'

I thought that might be going a bit far, but Tina didn't notice. She wanted to see Marty, and she wanted to see him now. She made me phone up to use my influence and make an appointment. Her mouth turned down ominously when she heard that it would be in two days, but she was consoled when I told her that Marty was kept busy seeing royalty of all nations.

After the phone call, she lost interest in me. She lay down, lost in her world of private sorrows and the intransigent English.

'About David?' I said.

'Don't talk to me about him,' she said.

'You said you wished we'd all leave you alone,' I said. 'Has somebody else been bothering you?'

'I'm a sick woman,' she said. 'I cannot tolerate this. Two men first, and now you. Leave me alone.'

'What sort of men?' I asked.

'Do you think I bothered to look? Unpleasant men. Men without manners who hustled into my apartment as if they owned it.'

'And did you tell them anything?' I asked.

'Like what?'

'Like where David is?'

'No,' she said. 'Why should I?'

'Why protect him?' I said. 'After what he did to you. By the way, what was it he did?'

'That, you ask? Well, I'll tell you. I'll tell the world. He treated me like a sucker. Followed me around like a lost dog. Played my heartstrings for his mixed up South African background. And then, one day he's off … no goodbye, no thank you sweetheart.'

'Was he acting scared?' I said.

'I guess he was nervous. Now I know why … the coward was

getting ready to dump me.'

'When was this?' I asked.

'Monday,' she said. 'I was never interested in him. He can stick it. So can you.'

It didn't look like there was any point in staying, and anyway my qualms were catching up with me. Tina Schoenberg met life as its victim and I didn't like the way I'd colluded with her, playing the thwarted woman to match her. I got up to go.

She didn't acknowledge my movement, so I was surprised when I heard her calling my name. I turned back to see her reaching into the pocket of her towelling robe. She pulled out a scrap of paper. I wondered whether she carried it with her wherever she went. I glanced at it as she held it at arm's length. There were no words on the paper, just a London phone number. I memorised it quickly before she withdrew it. I thanked her and said goodbye. All I got was an uninterested shake of the head.

I didn't have time for the massage. I got dressed. On the way out, I stopped at the desk. I rifled through the membership books when the receptionist left to answer the complicated inquiry about obligatory heat temperatures I'd thrown at her. Tina Schoenberg's name was there. I copied her address and checked the phone number against the one that Tina had given me. They didn't match.

I filed the two numbers in my head, to be dealt with later, and made my way through Covent Garden. I felt like I'd been through a wringer, but it hadn't affected my timing. It was dead on two o'clock when I arrived at the coffee shop to meet Lowri.

I walked in and just missed hitting my head on the beautiful if badly placed hanging plant basket which serves as decoration in trendy quick food joints. Lowri was neatly framed by two evergreen ferns, but otherwise she looked fine. A bit unkempt perhaps, but fine. Her gray hair was cut short to frame her small face. Her smile was as open as ever. Lowri was the first person I had got to know in England and she was special to me. A journalist who actually enjoyed freelancing, she never seemed bothered by the pressures of deadlines or the peculiarities of editors.

'What's happening?' I said as we kissed each other. 'Had another hard night?'

Lowri tried to look indignant. She was going through one of

her promiscuous phases and I'd long ago given up following the details.

'It was my carpentry teacher,' she said. 'She's been dropping hints for so long, and last night I got drunk with her and couldn't see any reason to refuse.'

'Passionate to the last, I see. So how was it?'

'I regret it. I woke up and didn't feel like talking to her. I mean, she's always going on about varnish. It's tedious first thing in the morning. I know it was all a mistake. It's going to make me feel very awkward in my class.'

'Wait a minute,' I said. 'You've been listening to her talking about varnish for quite a while. And all of a sudden you're bored with it. Bit of an overnight transformation, don't you think?'

She gave me something between a smile and a look of defiance.

'I'm allowed to change my mind,' she said. She put a stop to any more speculation by reaching into her packed bag and withdrawing the dreaded article.

We both gulped. The article had been an experiment for the two of us. It was an overview of the lives of London jazz musicians, and we'd planned to do it in what we'd thought was a flash of inspiration. It turned out to be a big mistake, and it says something for our friendship that we were still on speaking terms. As we did our research, which had involved an uncontrollable number of interviews, things had gone fine. They had also gone on and on and on. With two of us on the job, neither had taken control, and it had seemed easier to keep on talking. It had been interesting to get a glimpse of different London neighbourhoods — almost like flat hunting without the frustration — and we'd had some good conversations in our endless travelling from place to place. But we couldn't keep it up forever. Eventually we realised that we'd have to get it all on paper, and that's when the trouble had really begun. Our styles had clashed, and our voices risen. When we finally reached the last full stop, we had gone through it once again and pushed it out to the world. Unfortunately, the world seemed to have pushed it back, and we gloomily prepared ourselves for the agony again.

In fact, we needn't have worried. The editor had done a competent subbing job, and the article wasn't half as bad as our imaginations had made it. We put in one small change, just to prove that we'd read it, and then we sat back and relaxed.

We talked about memorable incidents in our common past and then turned back to the present. Lowri tried hard but failed to explain the dynamics of her search for a permanent relationship, since this was combined with a flight from anything even vaguely serious and so tended to make for confusion. I teased her about it, which she tolerated before getting her own back.

'I might be crazy on that score,' she said. 'But look at the saga of you and your career. I agree it's about time you moved out of the freelance racket. But do you think that being part of those humourless people in AER is progress?'

'It's a job,' I said.

'Uhmm.'

'It interests me,' I said. 'And maybe I'm working something out along the way. You know I wouldn't have minded working at AER.'

'So why didn't you?' she asked.

'Because they never seemed to take my hints. And, I suppose, because I wondered about my motives in attaching myself to an all-men operation. But who knows what would have happened if they'd asked? Anyway, they hired Bill Haskers instead. Not that he lasted long.'

Lowri threw me a long hard look. She seemed to be weighing something up, trying to find the best way to say it.

'You should go see him,' she said at last.

'Who, Bill? I heard he wasn't in such a good state. That was why he left.'

'He isn't,' she said. 'Nobody I know sees anything of him anymore. But you should go talk to him. I know he's got a reputation for being difficult, but he is good at his work. I heard there was a lot of tension about his leaving. I think you should talk to him — if only to rid yourself of your need to be accepted at AER.'

'Tell me more,' I said.

She shook her head. 'It's just gossip. Nothing I can pinpoint. I don't like to spread rumours, given what's happened. But go see him.'

She wrote out Bill's address for me and then changed the subject.

I let her — partly because Lowri, when not willing to talk, is un-pushable, and partly because I didn't know what to ask.

We both ordered salads of different descriptions, which were thrown on the table by an angry waitress. I looked at the food and thought I could guess what had contributed to her mood. Lowri and I managed to pick through them, pushing to one side the least identifiable contributions to the plate. By three, we were ready to go. We paid and walked to the tube, where we parted.

7.

Diana Nicholson lived in a ritzy flat near Belsize Park tube. It had its own ground-floor entrance and carpeting in the hall which was so deep that it made walking tedious. I was shown into the living-room, which lead out onto a large garden, and left there. The room had been furnished with an opulence that verged on the boastful. Two deep cushioned beige sofas faced each other across a Persian rug which, on its own, must have justified the burglar alarm I'd spotted outside. The heaviness of these items was offset by a sprinkling of side tables and easy chairs, all modern Italian, all modelled together with precision. On the mantelpiece a gold-rimmed mirror enlarged the already enormous room. A picture was wedged in one of its corners: a wedding photo. Tim Nicholson smiled brightly out of it, his arm around a woman who looked like she'd got everything she ever wanted.

She came through the French doors. Against the sunlight, she almost shone. She was dressed with a simplicity of style that showed her class. The yellow shirt and brown trousers bore no designer's name, but plainly they hadn't been picked off a rail. They were planned to complement her wavy blond hair and tanned skin, and they succeeded.

She looked almost exactly the same as she had in the picture, except for one detail. She was no longer happy. Small lines had begun to gather at the sides of her blue eyes, and her lips were pressed so tightly together that the strain showed halfway up her jaw. Without a word, she sat down on one of the couches and gestured me to the other. I complied.

'What can I do for you?' she said. 'I gather from Elsa that you said it was urgent.'

'It's about Tim,' I said.

'Tim who?' she asked. It was a question without curiosity. I knew she was talking to hide the nervousness, and she knew that I knew. She took a cigarette from the case beside her. A compact gold lighter set it on fire: her hands trembled as she inhaled.

'Tim Nicholson', I said, 'Your husband.'

'We're separated,' she said. 'Not divorced.'

'You didn't feel like coming to the funeral?' I said.

'What I do or do not feel is hardly any concern of yours. I have little time to spare and I suggest you get to the point quickly.'

'I'm interested in locating Tim's will,' I said.

She inspected the cigarette as if she didn't know how it had got into her hand. Then she lowered it and ground it to shreds in the thick glass ashtray. She didn't speak.

'Do you know where it is?' I said. 'Somebody suggested that you might.'

'Somebody was wrong.' It was said calmly enough, but there was a flash of panic in her eyes. 'I suggest you try his solicitor. Now, if that is all?'

'Not quite', I said. 'What were you and Tim arguing about on Friday?'

'I don't know what you're talking about,' she said.

'Come on, Diana,' I said. 'You must remember that somebody interrupted you. I could easily get him to identify you.'

This time she got out of her chair altogether.

'You have no authority,' she said. 'I do not have to answer your questions. If you wish to contact me again, do so through my solicitor.'

'What's his name?' I said.

'Slick. Robert Slick. I am sure you can locate him in the telephone directory.'

'I've had the pleasure,' I said. 'Interestingly, he was Tim's solicitor.' She didn't respond.

'What goes on between Robert Slick and Tim's mother?' I asked.

She glided to the door and held it open.

'I cannot see that that has anything to do with you,' she said. 'If you do not remove yourself, I will call the police.'

She meant it. I had no choice, so I walked towards the door. On the way I glanced at the hall telephone. I would have stopped dead, if she hadn't been behind to push me. I recognised that number. It was the one that Tina Schoenberg had just given me. The one where David was staying.

Back in Islington the tiredness that I'd fought off all week swept over me. It was Friday afternoon, the fourth day of my investigation, and all I'd collected were questions without answers. I walked into the kitchen where Sam was deep at work grinding an assortment of Indian spices.

'We haven't seen any films lately,' I said.

'Mmm,' he said.

'What about the one on at the Screen. Sounds like your taste — heavy, intellectual and full of meaning. Maybe we could catch the five o'clock.'

'Sure thing,' he said, 'Matthew can write an interpretation of it afterwards. Tony sent you the *Street Times*. Why don't you go through them. See if you can find any clues.'

They were stacked on the desk: six months' worth, with each issue containing five pages of lonely hearts ads. I sat down, swivelled the chair round and gazed at the ceiling. Matthew bounded into the room.

'I'll help,' he said.

'I don't think so. You need to read quite well.'

He jumped on my lap and biffed me in the nose.

'I can read,' he shouted. 'Can, can, can ... and I know how to spell that.'

'But Matthew ...'

I'd hurt his feelings. He climbed off and walked to the door, stopping only to fix me with an evil glare.

'You never let me have any fun,' he growled.

I gave in, called him over and sat him down.

'Go through these,' I said. 'Look for the words PLAYS, EYES, BLUE and SEEKS. Can you do that?'

'Of course,' he said. 'I'll find them.'

I went to the sitting-room and tried to sit. I didn't get far. Within a few seconds Matthew was standing in front of me.

'How do you spell ice?' he said.

I sighed and took him through it again. This time I wrote them out for him large and square and left him to it.

I must have fallen asleep. The next thing I knew was that Matthew was yelling in my ears.

'I've found one,' he shouted, thrusting a copy of *Street Times* in front of my face.

He was pointing at an article headlined 'Council in Ice Row'. I read through it. It was a complicated story which detailed how a councillor up north had made money by selling ice from the local morgue fridges. I shook my head at Matthew, and he went out of the room, disconsolate.

I assumed that would be the last of it, but five minutes later he was back again.

'I've done it,' he said, thrusting the same copy at me.

Thinking that I'd better put a stop to this game very soon, I looked where he pointed. And looked again.

'Male, Mars in Pisces, keen on jogging, gray eyes, seeks meeting,' it read.

That shook me out of my trance and I joined Matthew in the search. It wasn't that easy. Matthew took as deadly insult my attempt to check the magazines he'd already discarded, and I had to bribe them from his grip. By five, we'd covered the lot. We'd found six Mars in Pisces whose eyes oscillated between brown, gray and blue and whose interests covered most of the major sports. The karate-loving brown-eyed male from Tim's desk had called for a meeting on 5 June, almost two weeks before he was found dead.

I reached for the phone, dialled the *Street Times*'s number and asked for Tony.

'Hello,' I said, 'it's Kate. I've got those box numbers I wanted traced. I'll read them out to you.'

Before I could start, Tony's voice cut in. There was more than a tinge of hesitation in it, and my heart sank.

'Hold on a minute,' he said. The phone went dead.

I experienced two minutes of severe disappointment. Something had happened — just when I'd found a clue. I prepared myself for the worst. So when Tony's voice came back, strong and more grounded, I kicked myself for living in an internal disaster movie.

'Had to move phones so I wouldn't be overheard. I dropped a quiet word about the box numbers, only to find they're in turmoil in the advertising department. A subscriber complained that the staff had released his address.'

'When was this?' I asked.

'Some time during the last two weeks. A man complained to the management, and they'll use any excuse to come down hard on us. As a result, they've gone and set up a whole new security system which, funnily enough, also makes it more difficult for the advertising staff to leave early. Odd how these things always connect.'

'And I thought you had a liberal employer,' I said. 'I suppose this means I can't try out my box numbers?'

I'd reckoned without the spirit of rebellion amongst the *Street Times* staff.

'On the contrary,' Tony said. 'Why should we let them get away with this? We've worked out a new improved way of breaking the system. This one even gives us access to the more recent ads which used to be impossible. Give me the numbers we can test to see if it works properly.'

'That's great,' I said. 'Here you go: Jan 4, 213; Mar 1, 72; Mar 4, 119; May 3, 165; and Jun 1, 374. See what you can find with those. I'll ring back later.'

'Why don't we go for a drink instead?' Tony asked. 'I'm going to be in Islington this evening. How about seven o'clock at the pub around the corner from Sam's flat?'

'Fine,' I said. 'And, Tony, thanks a lot.'

'Not at all. It's done me a favour,' he said as he hung up.

We passed the time until seven by fooling around on bikes. Or, to be more accurate, Matthew fooled on the bikes while Sam and I played dumb posts around him. By the time we were ready for the pub, he'd only nicked my ankle three times. I didn't count the times he ran over my shoes.

In the pub garden, Tony was seated next to a small blond woman. Arranged under a tree, they looked a picturesque sight.

There was an air of expectation between them, a sort of atmosphere of interrupted intimacy. With her flowing black skirt and pink ruffled blouse affair, she was a woman who played to her own compactness. Light-brown eyes gazed brightly over her snub nose to offset the slight sharpness of her chin. Beside her, Tony, with his crisp white shirt unbuttoned at the collar, seemed to have lost some of his habitual sloppiness — along with his nervousness. He relaxed in his chair as he placed a delicately boned arm around her shoulders and introduced her as 'Caroline, who works in the advertising department.' I thought I understood the edge of keenness in his voice when he'd talked about cracking the box number system.

There was an awkward interval while we tried to place one another. Caroline and I skirted each other's lives, with Tony looking somewhat proudly on. We found a few people in common and exchanged desultory information about them. I'm never sure whether I'm altogether pleased to find out that everybody I meet knows everybody I've met, but it does make the conversation easier. By the time that Sam came back from his enforced expedition to the swings, we'd exhausted all avenues.

'So, what about the box numbers?' I asked. 'Did you manage to trace them?'

Tony smiled proudly and moved his hand lightly against Caroline's neck. She half jumped away, half moved into the curve of it, in response.

'We've worked out a great system,' Tony said. 'Or Caroline has.'

'How's it gone in practice?' I asked.

'Perfect. It's a matter of cracking the cross-referencing system they set up to stop us having access to the information. Actually, it's not only us … they instituted it ever since the time when somebody was found using the column to sell off stolen goods. We had the police crawling round the office, nosing about in the files. It was like the time when …'

'Tony.' To my relief, the reproof in Caroline's voice stopped him.

He straightened his backbone along with his thoughts.

'Those adverts are odd,' he said. 'They weren't taken out by one person. In fact your friend paid for the last one,' he said.

'My friend?'

'Yeah, Tim. Tim Nicholson. Did you know he's dead?' Tony leaned forwards towards me. 'Hey, this isn't connected to his death is it? I mean, I, we, don't want to get into anything too heavy.'

'I'll fill you in later,' I said. 'Don't worry, I'm only after information. Who took out the other adverts?'

Caroline, abandoned by Tony's arms, was looking lost. She jumped into the conversation.

'It was a South African,' she said. 'He said his name was Jonathan De Vries, but I know that was a lie because …'

Tony couldn't stay passive. He leaned forward. 'Yeah, he created hell over the fact that we released his address, but all the time he was lying to us … '

He stopped. No marks for interruption, he realised, and sort of mumbled into his drink.

I saw Caroline throw him a hurt look before she continued. 'You see, when he came to complain about the ads, he was acting funny, sort of frantic and worried. On his way out he pulled something from his wallet and the whole lot fell on the floor. I saw his driving licence.'

'And?' I said.

'And his name wasn't Jonathan. It was David Munger.'

'Are you sure?' I asked.

'Yes. I even saw a library ticket made out in that name.'

'Did you notice anything else?'

'Only the money,' she said. 'I've never seen so much in one wallet. Nearly all fifty-pound notes. Come to think of it, he always paid for the ads in cash and always in person.'

'But you didn't get his address?' I asked.

'No, sorry, like I said, I just helped him pick the lot up. I did notice that the ticket was for Camden libraries. That won't help much, will it?'

I left the question unanswered as Tony, who'd been making a strenuous effort to contain himself throughout the exchange, couldn't keep quiet any longer. He reclaimed Caroline's shoulder, turning her towards him as he faced me.

'What's going on? How come you're so interested in all this?' he asked.

I decided it was better to tell them and swear them to secrecy than to have their speculations doing the rounds. So I took a breath and started. Between the two of us, Sam and I managed to give them the guts of what had happened without indulging in excess details or back-tracking. The fact that I now had the mysterious David's surname didn't make it any the more comprehensible. When we'd finished, they both shifted uncomfortably in their seats. Caroline was the first to speak.

'But why? I suppose that's a stupid thing to say. You're trying to find out why. What I mean is why, if Tim knew David — that girl told you they were arguing in the Lock — why were they both taking out similar adverts?'

'Who knows?' I shrugged. 'What makes even less sense is where this all fits into Tim's death. I assume the ads were arranging meetings. But who was meeting whom? Never mind why.'

'I've got it,' Sam broke the silence. 'It was a secret society made up of ex-public school boys who met to discuss school things and Tim formed a splinter group and rewrote his will. So he was killed for factionalism.'

We all laughed but that didn't help.

'Who searched Tim's desk and why?' Tony asked.

'And why does a bird fly?' Matthew had returned from the swings and he recognised a game he played well.

'And why do you walk?' I asked.

He got an impish smile on his face. 'And why do ants trumpet?'

I fell for it. 'Do ants trumpet?' I asked.

Sam put a stop to what could have turned out to be a lengthy discussion.

'Hold on you two,' he said. 'Let's go eat.'

The five of us spent a while sorting out the car arrangements before we drove to the local Italian restaurant. The food was passable and the conversation relaxed. I felt pleasantly at ease after we separated from Tony and Caroline and dumped a sleeping Matthew into his bed. Sam and I sat by the television, coffee and brandy in hand. We got involved in a stoned argument about whether Tony and Caroline were going to sleep together or already had. In the end, we agreed that Caroline's reproachful look at Tony, combined with his eagerness for equal shares of glory, were proof enough that they had. That gave us ideas and we moved into the bedroom.

8.

I hadn't planned to work on Saturday. The postman changed my mind. He rang Sam's bell at eight and got me to sign for an anonymous manilla envelope that looked about as exciting as a subs request for *Soviet Weekly*. I opened it and pulled out the slim document that it contained. And I found myself holding not a copy, but the genuine article — the last will and testimony of Timothy Christopher Nicholson. The will was signed and dated. It had been drawn up four years previously and been witnessed by two people I'd never heard of.

I shook the envelope searching for a clue. There wasn't any. It had been registered in Camden Town but the sender had preferred to remain unknown. I turned to the document.

It didn't take long to read. The language was overblown and legalistic, but its basic message was simple. The bulk of Tim's estate he left to his wife, Diana Nicholson *née* Glovet. That aside, Tim had willed a few named items to his mother. The document was at pains to point out that they'd been bought with money Tim had earned rather than inherited.

That was it. Nothing spectacular, except in the way it presented a Tim of times gone by: a married man who'd left his fortune in his family. The will did nothing to answer the questions that I'd collected over the last week.

At one minute past nine, I dialled the number of Slick and Stevens. I spoke to the emergency service. A patient voice withstood my explanations and my bullying without giving anything away. In the end, I gave in, and left my number.

Within ten minutes, the phone rang. I picked it up to hear the honeyed voice of Robert Slick.

'Miss Baeier,' he said. 'Your message has been passed on to me. I understand that you have in your possession documents which may be of interest to me?

'Tim's will,' I said.

'Perhaps you realise that the possession of a will is a sacred trust and should not be violated. I hope you have not been as indiscreet as to read it?'

'I'm afraid so,' I said.

'That was unwise,' he said, and there was menace in his voice. 'I shall have to consider reporting this infringement to the relevant authorities, and the validity of the will may well be reconsidered.'

'Consider away. We both know that nobody can prosecute me for reading a document that was sent to me. What have you got against Diana Nicholson anyway?'

'What do you mean?' he snapped.

'Well, if you question the validity of the will, she'll lose all that money,' I said.

There was a pause and after it a transformation. Robert Slick changed gear. The passionless tones of an efficient lawyer returned.

'Well, perhaps we can call it a mistake on your part,' he said. 'If you would be so good as to return the will − by recorded delivery, of course − we can forget the whole matter.'

'I'd rather give it to you. This document seems to have a habit of getting lost,' I said.

He was annoyed, but he tried not to show it. 'Very well. I'll meet you at my premises in precisely one hour.'

He was waiting outside the Bond Street offices when I arrived. Without a word, he held out his hand to me.

'I'd like a receipt,' I said.

He reached into his weekend tweed and removed a set of keys which were held together by a link of hefty silver. He used them on the triple locks of the heavy door. He gestured me in.

'Wait here,' he said. 'I'll obtain the necessary paperwork.'

He wasn't gone for long. When he returned he thrust an envelope into my hand and then stood to one side to let me out.

'Wait a minute,' I said. 'I've got a couple of questions.'

'Miss Baeier, it is Saturday and I am expecting guests. Furthermore,

I have no brief to give you legal advice. Kindly consult another firm.'

'I hadn't noticed you being so fussy about your clients before,' I said.

'What are you implying?' he asked. The keys jingled impatiently in his hand; an emerald cufflink was roughly straightened.

'I mean that it seems odd you represented both Tim and Diana Nicholson. Given the amount of money involved, surely that is rather unorthodox?'

'Since you so unwisely read the will, I think you can see as well as I that Timothy did not consider it a conflict of interest,' he said.

'So you say,' I said. 'But that's what's odd. This will is four years old. That means it was drawn up when the two of them were still together. Surely, as Tim's solicitor you should have advised him to reconsider his will? I didn't know him then, but from what I've pieced together, he changed a lot in the last few years.'

I looked him in the eyes. It took some effort. His bland features had been transformed, and fury stared out at me. He looked like he was trying to conceal some inner force that was threatening to explode. His mouth twitched, a red flush tinged his face.

'Your type got to him,' he hissed.

'What type is that?' I said.

'Filth, rabble-rousers and filth. Undermining the very foundations of our society. Dissolute youth who have no families to speak of and try to drag everybody down to their own level. People of no stature …'

He caught himself and stopped. As the red went out of his cheeks, it was replaced by a looked of sadness. There was something familiar about it, but before I could think why, this, too was wiped out. The Bond Street solicitor had returned to this shell.

'Did Tim change his will?' I said.

'You have taken up sufficient time,' he replied, a smile on this face. 'Will you please vacate my premises?'

I had no choice. I left him there, standing under a remote painting of an idyllic countryside scene.

I walked up Oxford Street. My progress was slow, partly because Robert Slick's actions had confused me, and partly because of the sheer numbers of people that crowded the pavements. I thought about Tim and the life he'd rejected. By the time I arrived at Tottenham Court Road, I had regained most of my composure: enough to feel irritated by the consumerist orgy that was taking place around me. I bought a ticket to Belsize Park and spent the wait and the journey reading the adverts around me. I didn't learn much.

Diana Nicholson opened the door herself. She looked at me without speaking and then tried to slam it again. I stuck my foot in the gap. She gave in, and showed me into the living-room.

She exuded an air of nervous energy and the room had been punished for it. Everything in it was slightly off-balance — the glossy books lay open, tossed aside by a bored reader. The ashtrays overflowed and the room smelt stale despite the open French doors. I sat down and looked at her as she stood beside the window. She was a wreck. Dark shadows pressed against her eyes, accentuated by a run of mascara which trickled down their sides. Her fair hair was in disarray. I understood why, when she lifted her right hand and pulled it along her cheek to the back of her ear.

'I got the will,' I said.

'It has nothing to do with me,' she said.

'It leaves you the money,' I said.

'And you think that means so much? You're just like Tim … he never understood that I wasn't as concerned with money as he wanted to make out.'

'It means something to Robert Slick,' I said.

That broke the ice. She gave a laugh that started in genuine amusement but was headed out of control. She stopped herself in time.

'Poor Robert,' she said.

'Why?'

'He has some … problems,' she said. 'Not that I'd expect you to sympathise with the problems of the rich.'

'Try me,' I said.

She opened her mouth, and for a moment it looked like she was about to speak. Instead, her top teeth clamped onto her bottom lip and worried at it. A sliver of glossy skin detached itself and stuck to the end of one of her compact front teeth.

'It has nothing to do with you,' she said. 'Can't you leave the past alone?'

84

'What about the present? Tell me about David Munger,' I said.

'But that's what he …' she started. Then the animation was forced out of her voice. 'I don't know what you're talking about.'

'Someone gave me this number for David,' I said.

'Somebody was mistaken,' she said. 'I don't know a David Munger.'

'Is that what Tim and you were fighting about?' I asked.

'Why on earth should we? I have already told you, I don't know him. And I see no reason to continue discussing Tim with you.'

'Let's talk about the will, then,' I said. 'You're going to inherit quite a bit.'

'It might have slipped your notice, but I have money. I work for my living and do moderately well. Mother helps every now and then.' She sat down abruptly and reached for a pack of cigarettes. It was empty. Without looking at it she crumpled it in her fist and let it drop. She carried on talking, and as she did, her voice rose. 'And I don't care what you heard from Tim. I cared for him in a way he could never understand. It all went wrong when we saw each other, but I did care.'

'So, why did you split up?' I asked.

Tears rolled down her cheeks. They did it quietly and she left them to their work. But as they slid down, they drew what remained of her poise with them. Her face crumpled, her mouth puckered.

'I don't want his money,' she said. 'I never did. He just said that's all I was interested in because he felt guilty about the way he left me. It wasn't my fault. I know he changed. But he didn't give me a chance to adjust. And then he tried to say it was all my fault. Well, I had to keep my self-respect while he buried himself in his social whirl. He needn't have rejected me, too … I told him that.'

It was said through tears but she was holding something back.

'Where does David Munger fit in?' I asked.

She stood up and roughly wiped the tears from one cheek. The vulnerability that had crept into her face vanished.

'I don't know what you're talking about,' she said. 'Leave my house or I'll call the police.'

'This is getting repetitive,' I said.

'Well, then kindly leave and you'll no longer be bored by my actions,' she stuttered. She looked furious. I felt bad that I hadn't trusted her grief, but there was no way to tell her that. Instead, I did as she asked.

I was walking towards the tube when a white BMW convertible hissed passed me. I turned to watch its progress. It didn't go far. Within seconds it slowed down and parked outside Diana's door. A man got out. I recognised him. It was Robert Slick.

What had started as a warm day had turned out almost hot. I found a phone box and rang Anna. We spoke for a while before agreeing to meet. I sauntered across to Hampstead Heath, stopping on the way to pick up a handful of rolls, butter and some proscuito, half a pound of tomatoes and a couple of almost unbelievably shiny red apples. By the time I arrived at the women's pool, Anna was waiting, a spare bikini in her hand. I changed, spending some time working out how to contract the bottoms while I expanded the top. Instead, I decided to discard the top, then joined Anna stretched out on the grass. We sat in the sun and ate. The apples didn't fulfil their promise.

Muted conversations drifted over from where knots of women lay and talked. In front of us, four ducklings floated on the greenish water, their survival techniques perfect as they avoided the splash of intruders on their patch. I gave the pool one round trip before I was driven out by the cold. The icy shock did its work. By two o'clock I was almost relaxed.

We got dressed and into Anna's car. The tail ends of my hair dripped down my back; the murk from the water clung to my skin. We arrived at Cardozo Road and tossed for it. I got the shower, and Anna the bath. After that we went and sat in the garden, drinking coffee while we encouraged Daniel in his blitz on the encroaching weeds. Time slowed. At last it felt like a week of detection could look after itself.

By five we'd started on the tequila. By six, when Matthew and Sam arrived, I was even grinning. Sam sank wearily into a chair while Matthew did the rounds of the garden.

The sun was disappearing, leaving the sky a faded pink, by the time we discussed supper. We decided on a trip to the local Chinese for a Peking duck and pancakes.

We were in the middle of eating when the phone rang. Matthew, full up and looking for diversion, went to answer.

'No,' he said, his habitual telephone opening gambit. And then again 'No', followed by 'My mummy isn't here, I'm with Sam.' There was a pause and then he spoke again. 'This isn't her home,' he said. 'She lives in Dalston.'

'Who's that?' Anna asked as Matthew made to hang up.

'A man ... for Kate but this isn't her number,' he said.

I ran to the phone and grabbed it just before he reached the disconnection button.

'Hello,' I said, and then to Matthew, 'But you can see me in the room.'

'Kate?' Michael Parsons asked.

'I'm bored,' said Matthew and lunged for my hands.

'Get off,' I said. 'Sorry, Michael, bit of tackling going on here.'

'I'd like to see you,' Michael said.

'I want to play with you,' Matthew said.

'I can't stand it,' I said. 'Wait a minute. Okay, let's make a date,' I said down the line.

There was no answer.

'Michael?'

'Kate ... I'm waiting.'

'This is too much,' I said. 'How about making a date for tomorrow. Say five. At Sam's place.'

'I'll come then,' he said, and we broke the connection while Matthew made a bee-line for the laces on my sandals.

It took a while to extract him and even longer to persuade him to go to sleep. But eventually, through a carefully co-ordinated joint campaign, we succeeded. We settled down in the sitting-room, against the background of Eddice Cleanhead Vincent.

'So, what should I do, Kate?' Anna said, carrying on the conversation we'd had at the women's pool, as if there had been no interruption.

'About what?' Sam asked.

'Anna's had a new offer,' I said. 'To work for an all-women company. They've got a contract to make documentaries for Channel 4.'

'Sounds good,' Sam said. 'What's the problem?'

'The budget,' Anna answered. 'It's a group of film makers, all professional, who put in a proposal for a series, not thinking they had a chance. And now they've got the contract but not enough money. It'll be hell making the films to such tight amounts.'

'Maybe you should agree if they get the price upped,' I said.

'I've suggested that. But they don't dare. They're so delighted that they've even got a look-in. They want me to edit the whole series, and I'm worried it will be tedious.'

'Why tedious?' Sam asked.

'With the schedule they're on, I can't see them doing any in-depth research. It will only end up as an endless succession of talking heads — that's interviews, brought together in the cutting room.'

'Good to get away from the men in the television world, though,' I said.

'Oh, don't I know it! I've had them. I'm sick of being treated like a combination of the coffee lady and their mother who deals with all their shit.'

'So, what are the women like?' I asked.

'It varies. Some I've worked with before and would really like to again. Others are the type I know only too well ... you know, ones that pulled their way through the BBC without any help, and now that feminism has become a bit of a selling point they pay it lip service. But basically they made it too individually ... in their hearts they're convinced that anyone with merit can do what they want, and those that don't are only moaners. On the whole, I think the atmosphere would be so much healthier than my current living nightmare,' Anna said.

'It's hard to take,' Daniel said. 'That men are still so difficult. Isn't there any hope for us?'

'Depends on how much men try,' Anna replied. 'The ones I work with are at the pinnacle. There's really no reason for them to change, unless the women in their lives won't stand for it. What I can't make out is why the men that Kate works with haven't altered much. I mean, they've been around.'

As they looked at me expectantly, I almost went to the defence of the men at AER. I stopped myself and thought about why that was. I knew that a lot of my problems on freelance assignments for the organisation had come from my feelings of inadequacy and their insensitivity to it. They resisted anything that might alter the way they operated. I hated the way they worked together. They thought it was cosy. Or at least, Tim did. That's the word he'd once used to describe AER.

'I suppose I'm invested in it somehow,' I said. 'I've never really understood their behaviour.'

Sam snorted and then caught himself. 'Sorry, it's just that I hate it when you say that, Kate. It's about power, I'm convinced.'

'What, that they have all the power?' Daniel said.

'No, I was talking about Kate. I've always said this to her ... she thinks that if only she tried a bit harder, the atmosphere at AER would be better and they would accept her. I keep on trying to get it into her head how wrong that is. AER has managed to convince her that the difficulties are her fault. She's become the one that doesn't fit in, that behaves badly.'

'So, what can I do about it?' I asked.

'Nothing. That's exactly what I'm saying. Those men are too invested in their ways of being and it'll take more than you to change the way they relate. At the same time as you think yourself so weak, you take on the power and responsibility for the situation and play right into their hands.'

'Is that what I'm doing now?' I asked.

'Maybe,' said Sam. 'But maybe ... '

Anna interrupted. 'This could be different. You're not working so closely and perhaps you could use this as an opportunity to move away from their influence. I don't mean not work with them again; I mean not feel so tied into their problems as you seem to get.'

I let it hang there while I thought about it. I wanted to avoid the issue, just like I knew I'd avoided it for most of my working life. Although my political experience militated against it, I felt that within me there was something of what Anna had described in some of her new colleagues. As a journalist I had always worked in a man's world. It was a world that held many strong and active women, but still a world where men called the tune. When I thought about the experiences that my women friends in journalism underwent daily, I was able to see it clearly. But when it happened to me, I justified myself by finding other reasons. Perhaps I just didn't want to see myself in the role of a sucker.

'But doesn't this job mean I'm just helping them out of their problems again?' I asked Anna. 'I mean, talk about having to clean up their mess. Tim dies, there's some mystery involved, and here I am given the job of solving it, with almost no help from them.'

'At least you're realising it now,' she said. 'Treat this as a process where you can work something out for yourself.'

'And for a start, stop them phoning you all over the place. Who does Michael think he is, getting you on a Saturday night? And asking to see you tomorrow. He's not given any justification for it at all,' Sam said.

'Act one, scene one. The new Kate Baeier,' I said, as I reached for the telephone. I dialled Michael's number. His Saturday was not going well. He answered on the first ring with a voice risen in hope. I didn't have any illusions that he had been waiting for me. His voice dropped as he heard my name.

'I'd like to rearrange our date, Michael,' I said. 'Unless you can tell me if it is urgent, and why?'

He started to protest.

'It's the weekend,' I said. 'I'll see you on Monday. How about at the office?'

'Really, Kate, this is very inconvenient. And it's a bank holiday.'

'Well then, at Sam's place,' I said. 'Five o'clock.'

Michael gave in without much grace. I hung up, wondering whether it was all going to be as easy as that had been.

9.

Sunday morning I woke up on the edge of panic. I'd been dreaming that something large and all-enfolding was smothering me. I fought my way out of the dream and into consciousness. That didn't seem to help. I opened my eyes and identified the problem. It was Matthew, sitting on my head and reading a book. The book was upside down. Matthew was irritated when I told him so and more irritated when I pushed him off. I got dressed and set off to keep my appointment with Marty Succulent.

The streets were deserted. I made it to his Baker Street office in twenty minutes. I was admitted by one of his three fancy-looking receptionists and planted in the plush reception room to wait. Marty runs a smooth operation. He manages, more effectively than anybody else I've met, to partition off his working life. When he works, it's all work — Sundays are no barrier. For two weeks solid, he cracks, massages, stretches and needles his way through literally hundreds of bodies, and then he takes off for the rest of the month to Marbella, where he keeps his wife and two children in a luxurious, duty-free port. When I'd first met him, I'd taken Marty's glowing health as a tribute to his skill, but I've since realised that it probably owes more to his constant doses of sun.

Two years earlier, I'd crawled lopsided into his consulting rooms, only to be jerked back into place in the strictly limited fifteen minutes. Marty's expensive, but he's also skilled. Every now and then, I go back and get him to beat me into shape. Ever since he stopped trying to persuade me that he commutes from Spain because it's cheaper than living in the suburbs, we've developed an easy friendship.

'What's the matter with you?' he asked, eyeing me critically.

'Extreme rigidity, what else?'

He clucked his teeth as I lay down on the table. 'It's the same thing every time, Kate. And you know it. You didn't go and see that Alexander teacher I recommended, did you?'

I turned. 'I did, but I couldn't take him. He started into this sincere rap about transferring energy and learning kinesthetically and made me nervous. When I told him that, he got all intense and stared into my eyes, and that made me hysterical. So I left, muttering excuses about my back only needing a quick fix.'

'Well, what about trying rolfing?'

'Too much money, too much pain,' I said.

'You've done this to yourself and now you have to suffer to correct it,' Marty said, jerking me to prove his point.

'Come on, Marty, don't go all moral on me. How did you find Tina Schoenberg?'

'I assume you're not talking medically,' he said. Marty had spent hours filling me in on the private lives of his patients, but he hated to be taken for granted.

'Come on, Marty, I'm interested. What did you think of her?'

'Put it this way,' he answered, 'I wouldn't call her the most balanced of my patients. Guess what she thought she had?'

'Bilharzia,' I said. 'Did you find out anything about what she does in London?'

'Catching bilharzia, what else?' And he kneaded his fist slowly down my back.

'Look, I know you always manage to get them talking in here. It distracts them from the pain you cause. Does she work?'

'Slaves, according to her.' He was at the crown of my head, and I felt a sensation of pure relief as my neck stretched. 'Now turn over.'

'Where?' I asked.

'Onto your stomach,' he said.

'Where does she work?'

'At an embassy,' he said, to the accompaniment of a huge crack.

'Okay, I give in. What else did you learn?'

'She's tense,' he replied.

'I know that. Give, Marty, or I might outstay my welcome, and you don't want that, with all those rich patrons waiting for your services.'

'She works at the Argentine Embassy. She's got some sort of liaison job that she told me has very heavy responsibilities. Then she told me she was treated like nothing and ordered around. She lives on her own. Her boyfriend walked out on her and got involved with what she called an English aristocratic type with money.'

'Diana Nicholson,' I said.

'That could be it. I wasn't concentrating at the time. She has some very knotty vertebrae, brought on by early distortions in her external object environment.'

'What's this?' I said. 'Are you training to be a shrink?'

'As a matter of fact, I am thinking of expanding my training. I do so much lay therapy at the moment I may as well cash in on it. But apart from a preliminary assessment, I didn't really establish much about Tina Schoenberg except that she doesn't have bilharzia. Now relax, this is the last one.'

The last one turned out to be a real bone crunch, and after it I was turfed out. I paid my money, did a quick check on the numbers of diamonds in the waiting-room, and left.

Bill Haskers, the man who had joined AER and left within a space of a few months, lived in one of the many post-war concrete monsters that are dotted through Hackney. The neighbouring Hackney Downs only emphasised the sheer ugliness of the buildings. I found his block and climbed slowly up the cold dark stairs to the fourth floor. My steps echoed on the graffiti-covered walls. The landing was like a prison balcony: doors regimented along it.

I found number 94 and knocked. There was no reply. I pushed the heavy metal door, and it opened slightly. I knocked again. From inside I heard the sound of scraping, as if a record had finished and was circling aimlessly along its grooves.

Gingerly, I walked into the narrow hallway. Boxes of books and papers lined the wall, and revolutionary posters competed with the mould that was slowly gaining ascendancy. Clutching my jacket around me, I walked towards the sound.

The sound carried on as my eyes acclimatised to the dark gloom. Bill was by the window almost motionless. A cloth in his hand, he was methodically wiping at one small area. His whole body was concentrated into the work, almost as though he were trying to push the dirt out and through the pane. There was not sign that he had heard me or was ever going to acknowledge my presence.

'Bill?' my voice sounded pathetic.

He half turned towards me but left his hand to its perpetual motion. He blinked his half-closed eyes at me as if trying to place me.

'I know you,' he said. 'Kate Baeier. Hello and goodbye.'

'I'd like to talk to you,' I said.

'Who wouldn't? My mother, Milly, my so called friends and now you. I don't even know you ... just your face from one of those parties where everybody smiles and nobody is amused.'

'They can be bad,' I said. 'Come and sit down for a minute. The window can wait.'

'I'm not so sure,' he said. But he put his cloth down and moved towards me. I sat on an old armchair. He leaned against the wall opposite and gazed at me between those half-closed lids. He had the look of a man drugged either by his doctor's prescription pad or his own grief. I guessed it must be a combination of the two. His narrow shoulders were stooped in a pose of self- protection. He'd shaved his mouse-brown beard off, and now his disappearing chin had nowhere to go and nowhere to hide.

'I've come to ask you about AER,' I said.

'Try again,' he said. 'That's not my favourite subject.'

'Tim's dead you know.'

'I heard. Pity. I liked him. But it'll come to all of us and some don't care if it does.'

'They think he might have been killed.'

'It's funny,' he said. 'The things people bring you to cheer you up. I've heard that one, too.'

'Why did you leave AER so quickly?' I asked.

'My information network's better than yours,' he responded. 'I thought it would be all over town. I couldn't take it and I showed it. Aldwyn says I ruined his filing system when I went on my binge of destruction. Aldwyn says a lot. But none of it means much. Tim said nothing and meant a lot.'

'What's that supposed to mean?' I asked.

He move away from me and back to his window. The cloth squeaked on the pane again. His words came as if from an enormous distance.

'Haven't you heard? I'm irrational. Nobody can help. Tim tried. But he couldn't. He trusted me, you see. Trusted me. Now he's dead.'

'Is there a connection between the two?' I asked.

'My analyst says I shouldn't try to make connections yet.'

'Don't you care who killed Tim?'

'My analyst says I shouldn't get into anger. My analyst says a lot. Funny, I thought they weren't supposed to speak. Suppose he has to fill the gaps somehow.' His shoulders shook. It wasn't amusement.

I turned to go. Just as I reached the door, his voice called me back.

'Sorry, Kate Baeier,' he said. 'I'm not always as bad as this. I'll come through.' Conviction ran very faintly through his voice.

'Tim gave me a document. Milly's got it. I hope it helps. Helpless hope.'

I pulled the door open, to be confronted by a large woman dressed in country tweeds. She had all Bill's colouring, but where he radiated depression, she projected a fierce cheeriness.

'Oh, I'm so sorry, I just popped out to the shops. You're one of William's friends, Miss ...?'

'Kate Baeier,' I said.

'How nice, and I'm William's mother. Mrs Haskers, but then you know that don't you?' She threw me a hollow laugh. 'Don't go, come into the kitchen, and we'll have a nice cup of tea.' Her voice dropped to a whisper, 'Our William's not entirely well.'

I thought this something of an understatement, but kept such ideas to myself. I was feeling trapped, but she wasn't going to let me escape. Before I could protest, I was swept into the kitchen and seated.

She kept up a steady stream of chatter as she busied herself in unpacking what looked like an endless range of biscuits. She concentrated on the evils of garden pests and she did it with gusto. On the way, she made a point of letting me know that there was money in the family. 'Not rich, of course, but enough to pay our rather efficient gardening help, although one has to do most things oneself.' On the subject of Bill, she was less self-assured.

'Do you think it's in our genes?' she said conversationally.

'He's just going through a hard time,' I replied. 'How long has he been so depressed?'

'Oh, you think he's depressed? From my side, he strikes one as rather violent, although of course that's only a mother's view. I can't actually say. He did ring us but I have been so busy. I had to take Charles to the airport on Monday, he does have so much responsibility with his business, and on Tuesday I had the Women's Institute. Wednesday was shopping, and of course Thursday is early closing, and since Friday was the end of the week, it was only yesterday that I was able to come down and look after the poor boy.'

I'd had enough. I had to get out and if it took rudeness, I was prepared for it. As I walked into the hall, Bill appeared. He thrust a grimy-looking paper at me.

'Milly's address,' he said.

'Now, William, don't worry your friend.' His mother turned to me.

'Oh dear Miss ... Cater isn't it. You haven't touched your tea perhaps you take sugar?'

I grinned weakly and mumbled my way out of the door. As I got to the stairs, I heard her voice ringing behind me.

'Come in now, William. She seemed a nice girl. I always thought that Milly — a common name isn't it? — was no good for you.'

After the cloying atmosphere of Bill's depression, even the Hackney air felt good. I got into my car, glanced at the paper that Bill had given me, and drove to Milly's Hampstead residence.

She answered the bell on the second ring. She was wearing a sort of peasant affair with lots of pieces and no focus. Chunky bracelets held her plump arms, and her long brown hair trailed heavily behind her. I introduced myself, and she showed me up to her attic room. The place was palatial but frozen, with *objets d'art* dotted around even the hall in a deliberate show of casualness. I looked around puzzled, trying to figure it out.

'I clean it,' she said.

'Oh?'

'It's not mine, I just get the room in exchange for cleaning the house. I'm on a nine till eleven shift. You're lucky, I've just finished.'

Her room was in a kind of friendly disorder that contrasted strongly with the rest of the house. In the middle, under the skylight, stood a long work desk, littered with half-finished earrings and miniscule tools. There were no chairs on the plain wooden floors. I sat on the end of the bed.

'I've just been to see Bill,' I said.

'Is he still bad?'

'Yeah, and his mother doesn't seem to be helping things much.'

'If you think she's the limit, you should meet his father. All he cares about are his precious stocks and shares and whether he's being ripped off by the grocer's delivery boy.'

'And Bill? Is he often that depressed?'

'He goes under sometimes, but this is the worst. I'm keeping away till his mother goes. When we're all together, we seem to

96

fight over him. I'm trying to get him over here, but she doesn't think it's right, living in other people's houses.'

'Bill said you had some papers that could help me. I'm trying to sort out what's going on at AER,' I said. Then I added, 'One place where Bill worked for a while,' as a look of confusion stirred her placid face.

'Oh, right. I don't go for that scene much − too intellectual for me. I like to work with my hands: it helps my karma.'

I nodded. 'The papers?'

She uncoiled herself from her lotus position and moved to a cupboard by the door. It took a while before she re-emerged, a foolscap notepad in hand.

'This must be it. He asked me to keep it safe. Somebody gave it to him. I looked through it. But it didn't make much sense to me. All about Argentina and generals and a whole list of dates and names.'

I thanked her and said I'd show myself out. I left her where she was, reseating herself with a look of peace carefully composed on her face.

I examined the notebook as soon as I got into the car. I didn't get much further than Milly had. It was about half filled by Tim's untidy scrawl, criss-crossed with lines and arrows and the occasional ring in red. Almost buried amongst the frantic marks were names: names of Argentinians high up in the junta. Some were easily recognisable; others I could only guess. But that wasn't all. The Spanish names were interspersed with people of a different heritage: South Africans, and plenty of them. They were familiar surnames, Afrikaans standards − but I couldn't fit a face to any of them.

The text ended abruptly with several exclamation marks to underline Tim's growing excitement. Then nothing. I turned to the back of the book and found, on the back cover, a list of telephone numbers. I remembered Tim's habit of losing telephone books, with the result that he collected numbers on anything he was writing. Only one number stood out and that's because it was written in red, slightly larger than the rest as if to proclaim its importance. Hugh Castlewitch, it read, followed by seven digits.

I drove to the nearest phone box and dialled the number. I got through to a booming voice on the other end. He wasn't pleased at my request. It sounded like I'd interrupted a raucous family lunch, but he agreed to see me.

A little boy answered my ring. A very precise little boy. Dressed in a pair of flannel shorts topped with a gray V-necked jumper, he looked like he'd just come out of a school concert. His straight, well-combed neat brown hair did little to contradict the impression. When Hugh Castlewitch came up behind him, the contrast was startling. For Hugh was a huge man, well over the six-foot mark, and he knew it. The creeping gray in his otherwise red hair only helped his imposing presence. He brushed the child away with a flick of his wrist on which more carrot hair rested.

'Come in,' he said. 'I can give you a few minutes.'

He led me into the study. It was the room of an old-fashioned scholar: all leather, mahogany and hidden lighting. Hugh's history belonged to the folklore of the anti-nuclear movement. As a physics graduate in the late 1940s, he had been in the right time and the right class to look set for a career which would eventually culminate in a new year's honours list. Instead, he'd halted his meteoric rise through the civil service by publicly expressing his doubts about nuclear weapons. He was now a well-established physics professor who ran a tight department, while he used his years of activity in CND to push back the more radical, feminist elements that were threatening to take over the organisation.

Hugh sat behind his polished desk and indicated an armchair which was arranged to one side of it. He reached into a cupboard and poured himself a Glenfiddich. He didn't offer me one.

'What can I do for you?' he asked and then lifted his head towards the door. 'What do you want? I told you not to interrupt when I'm working.'

I turned to the door. The little boy was there, shifting from one foot to the other.

'I just, I … mummy asked me to ask you if you wanted tea,' he stuttered.

'Can't you see I'm drinking?' Hugh boomed. 'Now please leave us alone.'

The boy scuttled out.

'Tim Nicholson had your name in a book,' I started.

Hugh drank a slug and put the glass down as if it was distasteful.

'That in itself is not unusual. As chairman,' he stressed the last syllable and looked at me for reaction before he continued, 'of a number of committees, I am often in demand. I don't usually work on Sunday though.'

'I'm sorry,' I said. I was beginning to identify with the little boy.

'It's done,' he said. 'Spit it out. As I always say: when in doubt, suck it and see.'

'What did Tim want from you?' I asked.

'He used to come to me for information. As do many other journalists. Sometimes I curse my career in physics, since it seems to have made me a goldmine for information seekers.'

'Must be tough,' I said. 'And they plead for you on committees?'

Hugh lifted his whisky again, gulped the rest of it and then threw back his head. His laughter filled the air.

'Forgive me,' he said. 'Can't stand family Sundays. Here, have a drink.'

He reached into the cabinet again and poured me one. He gave himself another, this time double the quantity.

'Tim Nicholson was an interesting boy. Misguided, verging on the ultra left, but a good worker. He used to consult me. The last time he came to see me he wanted to know about the manufacture of nuclear weapons. He was interested in knowing whether Argentina had the capacity for production.'

'And what did you say?'

'I told him, yes. Especially given the information he brought me.'

'Which was?'

'Are you not the Kate who has worked at African Economic Reports?' he asked.

I nodded.

'This is precisely what I find the new left lacks. Co-ordination. I prepared a paper which set out my findings for Tim. Of course he was never able to collect it. I gave it to that chappie, the other one that works at the organisation. He collected it, let me see, six days ago, I think.'

'Who was it?' I asked.

'The fellow was rather full of himself, well dressed for you AER crowd. He was in a hurry, we didn't get much chance to exchange life histories.'

'Aldwyn Potter,' I said.

'That's the one. Ask him about it and come back if you have any new questions.'

He rose and walked me to the door. On the way we passed the little boy, lurking in the corridor. I threw him a wink. He fled.

Aldwyn lived, along with his girlfriend Margaret, on two floors of a house located in one of the more genteel parts of Highgate. It's the kind of area where weeds don't exist and the garden gates shut with a twang which is supposed to scare off strangers. Rows of front gardens bloomed with a riot of colour, but even the popular azaleas had an air of the antiseptic about them.

When Aldwyn opened the door, I realised how perfectly he fitted into the scene. He was dressed in a pair of brown cords, a cream shirt unbuttoned at the collar, and a beige tank top to finish it off. His cream sneakers looked like they were sent to the dry cleaners regularly.

'Hi, Aldwyn,' I said. 'You're looking nice.'

'You said that the last time I saw you,' he accused. Pleasantries over, he showed me upstairs.

I looked over the kitchen, while Aldwyn busied himself with one of those percolators that make a lot of song and dance about producing a mediocre cup of coffee. They'd gone for a rural look: stripped-pine cupboards and rough white walls, and then spoiled it by replacing the windows with modern slots and the lights with neon. In the background came the sound of Mozart interspersed with the discreet patter of an electric typewriter.

The coffee machine gave a last spurt as the remnants of the brown liquid reached the top. Aldwyn poured some into two hefty-looking mugs and walked out. I followed. Margaret turned from her typing when we got into the sitting-room. We greeted each other, and then she made an excuse and retreated.

It was another room at odds with itself. The bottle-green sofa looked slightly sick against the fawn wall to wall, and the heavy velvet curtains blocked what must have been a splendid view. Aldwyn and I sat opposite each other on two mustard tubular and canvas efforts. His red hair clashed with them.

'I gather this isn't a social call, Kate,' he said. 'Actually, I am rather pleased you came. I was on the point of contacting you.'

'About what?' I said.

'I've given the matter lengthy consideration and have decided on balance, to speak my mind. I feel you should stop your inquiries. The police are satisfied, and I do not see why we should indulge in a further post mortem.'

'I've never seen you so impressed with the police before,' I said.

Aldwyn's mouth moved in an imitation of a contemptuous smile. I thought it looked a trifle strained around the edges. He didn't speak.

'I'm not stopping now,' I said. 'I owe it to myself. And, I think, to Tim.'

Aldwyn's chest swelled out, his eyes glared. I knew the symptoms. I was going to get a speech. But even knowing this, I was surprised at the subject he chose.

'Feminism has played an enormous role in the development of post-1970s politics. I would be the last to deny that,' he said. 'But I do sometimes have the feeling that some of you have become carried away by your initial successes. I must admit I am beginning to be rather tired by all those endless justifications in terms of personal development. Don't you understand how the real world works?'

I put my coffee down abruptly. I noticed my hands were shaking. I decided to ignore them.

'What's that supposed to mean?' I asked.

'Only that I cannot help wondering whether you haven't allowed yourself to become carried away,' Aldwyn replied.

'Like you carried away Hugh Castlewitch's conclusions?' I asked.

'I cannot see what that has to do with you,' he said. 'That work is property of African Economic Reports and has no bearing on anything else.'

'Tim was working on it. And he thought it important enough to ask Bill Haskers to hide the original research.'

'Well, doesn't that prove my point?' Aldwyn asked. He pulled the tank top over his flabby stomach.

'I don't get it', I said.

'Any sensible person would understand. Tim Nicholson and Bill

Haskers. Tim was, as I have already implied, inclined towards the conspiratorial, and as for Bill ... everybody knows he's not, how would one put it ... he's not completely compos mentis. Of course, that knowledge changes everything.'

'I don't see why,' I said. I didn't see why I was getting involved in a debate on mental health either, but I felt the urge to puncture some of Aldwyn's self-assurance. I knew it wouldn't get me anywhere. I changed tack before he could reply.

'Tell me about David Munger,' I said. 'Ever heard of him?'

Aldwyn gave a giggle. He stopped himself and transformed it into a manly belly laugh.

'You *have* become involved. Well, they do say paranoia is infectious,' he said, after he'd rumbled to a halt. 'Tim had a bee in his bonnet about David Munger. Absolute nonsense, I am assured of that.'

'Did Tim talk about David in the office?'

'He caused somewhat of a commotion ... that would be a more accurate way of putting it. David was one of our general contacts. Tim decided to focus his tensions on him. In fact, the more I contemplate it, the more certain I become that Tim was in a state of some nervous instability before he died. Which does lead me to the obvious conclusion ...' he left it in the air and glanced at me helpfully.

'What did Tim have against David?' I asked.

'Some nonsense about David looking through his private belongings. Of course, if Tim left his desk in its usual disorder, what could he expect? And, after all, David was merely searching for a telephone number. That hardly qualifies as a crime, don't you agree?'

'It depends,' I said. 'When did all this happen?'

'Earlier in the year. It didn't last long, as I expected. These things usually do blow over, if enough discretion and tact is employed. As far as I was concerned, when Michael returned from his holiday at the end of April, the matter had been dropped. Tim seemed to have calmed down. Until, of course, the weeks immediately preceding his death, when he became irrational once again.'

'Did Tim mention Tina Schoenberg?' I asked.

Aldwyn had lost interest. 'Never heard of her,' he said. 'You must understand that we at African Economic Reports prefer not to live in each other's pockets. Now, it is Sunday, so if you wouldn't mind?'

He hustled me out of the house and placed a restraining hand on my shoulder.

'I trust you will not misinterpret my words,' he said. 'I have nothing against women's liberation. In fact, I support it and always have done. I merely feel that it can be used as an excuse for anything.'

He let go, and I walked away. Behind me the gate clicked shut.

I was almost back at Sam's flat when I changed my mind and my direction. I turned off Upper Street and into the heart of Barnsbury. I found Zoe Fridenberg's house in a small cul-de-sac where the façades gleam white and traffic noise is just a distant memory. Zoe answered the door, her owlish eyes blinking behind the gold rims. She didn't seem too pleased to see me, but she showed me upstairs anyway.

We landed up in a large sitting-room. It had been furnished in the early 1960s, the time when Zoe had arrived from South Africa, and little had changed since then. The colours were brown and fawn, the curtains an overblown flower design. Several Makondes, ornate and tall, stood on the bookshelves which lined one side of the room. They gave the place almost its only life.

'What can I do for you Kate?' Zoe said. I was taken aback by her voice. I always was surprised by it. It had almost no depth, as if it were flipped out of her mouth from the middle of her throat.

'I've come round to give you this,' I said. 'I thought your friends might be interested.' I handed her the notebook that Milly had given me. Zoe looked through it, but it didn't mean anything to her and she soon got bored.

'What friends?' she asked, suspicion giving the voice a fraction more tone.

'Somebody in the ANC might be interested. It's the result of some research that Tim Nicholson was doing. Something to do with Argentina and South Africa.'

Zoe's lip parted a fraction. She threw me a slight smile that had derision written all over it.

'You were active in Portugal, weren't you?' she asked.

'Yes,' I said. I was getting confused.

'You were involved in various actions of a violent character?' she persisted.

I nodded. I couldn't see what she was getting at, but I knew from experience that there would be no way of short-circuiting her journey.

'We do not approve of such actions,' she said.

'I thought you were committed to armed struggle?'

'That's different. We have an organisation. We have politics. We strongly disapprove of individual action.'

'But you're talking of Portugal before the coup. There are cabinet ministers all over the world who've been part of armed struggles.'

'Nevertheless …' she said. She left the word in the air as if it spoke volumes. I suppose it did. Zoe came from an old-style party family, hard working, dedicated and tending to the inflexible. We'd brushed against each other's politics before. She thought I wasn't serious enough. I found her sanctimonious. She always acted like the struggle was being waged by her family on her territory, and anybody else would have to receive a written invitation.

I knew I wouldn't get any further without an explanation, so I filled her in. I told her about Tim's death and how he'd given the notepad to Bill Haskers. I told her about David Munger, his involvement with Diana Nicholson and his destroying my saxophone. And I ended with what Tina Schoenberg had told me: that two men were looking for David.

'Munger … the name rings a bell,' she said when I'd finished. 'I think he was one of those recently arrived students who dabbled in anti-apartheid circles. Not a serious man: I saw him at a couple of meetings, but he couldn't adjust to our democratic workstyle. He must have left for the excitement of your lot. It's always easier to criticise than stick with it day after day.'

I held my tongue. I knew that if I started to argue, we'd do the circle: we'd start in Africa, slip over to China and the Gang of Four, and then we'd be lost for a good few hours. I pointed at the notebook.

'Will you look into it?' I asked.

'I suppose it can't do any harm. We'll get in touch if anything comes up.'

For the rest of the day, I pretended I was having a weekend. I cooked lunch, and then fell asleep to the afternoon movie, waking up in time to catch the finale as three men in flying jackets headed for a black and white sunset. Sam took Matthew to his mother's, and then we went to the West End. I can't remember what we saw. All I know is that, for the closing scene, the sunset was in technicolour, and the airmen wore T-shirts.

10.

Monday was a bank holiday. The weather knew it. I woke to continuous gray drizzle and a curious hush. The hustle of neighbours rushing to work and the honks of the lorries in the nearby New North Road were muted. Nothing stirred except for the steady patter of the rain.

Ignoring Sam's protests, I dragged myself out of bed and into my clothes.

'Take the day off,' he muttered.

'Maybe later,' I said. 'I have the urge to go see Tina Schoenberg.'

'You and your urges. It was bad enough when you were working to a deadline, but now you've become a detectionaholic.'

'You didn't object to my urges last night,' I countered. 'And I do have a deadline. I was given ten days.'

'That's you all over, Kate. Do you think they'll remember the time-limit and stick to it?'

'I doubt it,' I said, 'but I'll try to.'

I had little trouble finding Tina's flat. Situated in one of those imposing St John's Wood blocks which was built in the 1920s, it just about overlooked Regents Park. The apartments are expensive, the type that charge a massive annual porterage fee, but my first impression was of darkness. The place had seen better days, and now it was stagnant. The luxurious hall carpet, a dull red, soaked up all the light along with the sound. I felt caged by the heavy brocade wallpaper as I climbed the stairs to Tina's third-floor flat. I reached her front door and rang the bell. A voice from inside yelled at me to hang on, or go away. I hung on. While I waited, the hall light finished its economic cycle and clicked off, leaving me in the dark. I felt my way along the wall until I found the switch and pressed it. At that moment, Tina opened her front door.

'What the hell are you doing?'

'Switching the light on. Waiting in the dark makes me feel like I'm about to be ice-picked,' I said.

She smiled. 'I know exactly what you mean. This place is gloomy.'

Her smile didn't last long. It was replaced by a look of profound dissatisfaction. 'Sorry I took so long but I was on the phone,' she said. 'It's the last straw − the orange squeezer won't work any more. I've had it.'

Her brown eyes glistened. I wondered whether she kept them that way to complement her vibrant complexion.

'I'll look at the squeezer,' I said. 'Maybe I could fix it.'

Before she had been blocking the doorway; now she lunged to get me inside. All I had to do was fix the dammed thing.

I was marched into the kitchen. It was a soulless room, designed by somebody who'd never have to cook in it. All the facilities − the double sink, the split-level cooker, the deep freeze − were there, but they were filed together almost without intervening work surfaces and certainly without love. If Tina had inherited this room, she hadn't bothered to put her mark on it.

She pointed to a table laden with gadgets. 'There it is. It's dead. What am I going to do?'

I made my way towards the table, trying to work out which was the dead orange squeezer. Eventually, I picked up the right one and turned the switch. Nothing happened.

'You see, it's not me: it's had it. What am I going to do?'

'Calm down,' I said. 'We already knew it wouldn't work, so don't panic. Why don't you sit down.'

I traced the cord, checked the machine was plugged in, and then gingerly turned it over. To be honest about this, I knew how Tina felt. I hate machines that don't work. I always try to fix them and I rarely succeed: all that happens is that I end up clutching my head and cursing the world for moving out of the stone age. The orange squeezer incident was no exception. By the time I'd bungled myself and a screwdriver through the plug to check the fuse and then put the whole thing back together again, I was irritated. Tina, who kept up a continual barrage of moans while I bit my lip, spoke up when I finally betrayed myself with a long-drawn-out curse.

'No need to get so uptight about it,' she said. 'It's only a machine.'

'Thanks a lot,' I said as I rotated it once more. 'What's this switch?'

'The safety mechanism. You can use batteries on the machine, so it has a switch which makes sure you don't turn it on by mistake. There's nothing wrong with this machine except that it doesn't work.'

I flicked the safety catch, plugged the machine in and watched it squeezing the air.

'Great, now all I need is some oranges. Are you walking my way?' Tina said.

'Hope not, I've just come in. I'd like a brief talk with you.'

She offered me a drink and led me to the sitting-room. It, too, was stale: a big room with solid mahogany furniture and thick musty curtains to match. Tina pointed in the direction of an elegant gray velvet armchair.

'That's the most comfortable seat, which doesn't mean much. This flat was passed on through another diplomat, and by the look of his taste in fittings, I'm glad I never met him.'

'How was your time with Marty?' I asked.

'I liked him. At least he took me seriously, which is more than most other so-called experts I've consulted. He paid attention to my liver line and I could tell how concerned he was. He put me on a vegetarian diet,' she said.

'Let's hope it works,' I said. 'I've come to ask you about David Munger.'

'I've told you everything I know.' Her face belied the lack of expression in her voice. A look had settled there: a look of embarrassment, or of fear.

'I think you've told me more, and less, than you know,' I commented.

She jerked her head up as if to protest, but she didn't get that far. Her head dropped again and she concentrated on the ruby ring that dwarfed her index finger.

'I don't know what you mean,' she said, without even an attempt to sound convincing.

'That number you gave me — where did you get it?'

'David gave it to me,' she mumbled. She twisted the ring hard.

'Why?' I asked. 'If he left you, why did he leave a number?'

'What has it got to do with you?' she shouted. 'My life is in tatters and you have to come and cross-question me. So what if he didn't give it to me. I found it. Go search around the other woman's private life.'

'Do you know who she is?'

'Diana something. What do I care? She can have him.'

'It's Nicholson,' I said. 'She used to be married to Tim Nicholson. Did you know him?'

She let go of her ring to stare at me. She went completely still. Only when she looked down and saw her hands hovering above her lap did she pulled herself out of her trance and clasp them together.

'Yes,' she said. 'I knew him. He introduced me to David. He came round.'

'Recently?' I said. 'Did you see him just before he died?'

'He visited me,' she said. 'He'd never done that before. I didn't know him very well. He wanted to know about David. He asked me questions and I told him about that woman, Diana. It wasn't my fault. I was upset. I wasn't doing anything wrong. What was I supposed to do?'

Tragedy had returned to Tina Schoenberg's face. I would have taken it more seriously if she hadn't looked so much as if she were enjoying it.

'What did Tim say when you gave him the number?' I asked.

She smiled, satisfied at the memory. 'He was furious. He said that David had gone too far. He said he'd get him.'

'Did you tell David?'

'Why shouldn't I?' she replied. 'I told him Tim had found him out and was going to get him. That got him worried, didn't it? Of course he tried to deny it.'

'Deny what?' I asked. I was confused.

'I thought you said you knew David. He would deny anything. He insulted me, but I knew I had him worried. He denied he was carrying on with that woman.'

'Where did you find her number?' I asked.

'His address book,' she said. 'Her name and number, ringed in red. I knew something was going on ... he had changed and wasn't interested in me. I hadn't done anything wrong and then I found the number ... I knew immediately. That's why I told Tim. I am not sorry. I, Tina Schoenberg, have nothing to apologise for. There is no reason why I should keep quiet. I gave Tim and you the number so that she could feel some of my pain. Let her be made miserable by David's behaviour.'

'And you have no other number for him?'

'I have an address,' she said. 'Here take it. Just leave me be. I never want to hear anything about David Munger in my life.'

I copied out the address she gave me and stood.

'One last thing,' I said. 'Where did David work?'

She laughed. It came out closer to a sneer. 'That man doesn't know the meaning of work. He was more interested in mine than in his. He worked occasionally for a news agency, International News Limited. But he didn't need money.'

I thanked her and left.

The address she had given me was at the back of King's Cross. I found it without much difficulty. A dingy street, a row of houses whose neglect was turning to decay, and nothing to distinguish number 58 from the rest. I parked near to it and sat in my car, wondering what next to do. I'd spent a week crossing, or missing, David Munger's path and now that I had almost found him, I felt nervous. I toyed with the idea of driving off for reinforcements, but apathy kept me where I was. Just at the point where I had persuaded myself that any move would be better than none, the door of the house opened.

A tall, fair-haired man stepped out. He was neither unconscious, nor in white face, but I would have recognised him anywhere. David Munger it was, and slickly dressed in a well-fitting gray business suit. He looked like a man with a purpose. I watched him close the door, take a set of keys from his jacket pocket and get into a dirty white mini.

I turned my key and waited, my head lowered. The mini brought back visions of my crushed alto, so when Munger pulled out abruptly and nearly hit a passing VW Estate, I was delighted. Unfortunately for my sense of natural justice, the VW driver was alert and after delivering a barrage of curses, drove off leaving the mini unscarred. I waited. Either David was an abysmal driver or his nerves were shot to hell. He made a few more attempts to pull out before he finally succeeded. He drove down the road, hugging the central white line. I followed.

He didn't drive far, which was lucky for me. The tracking business was harder than I expected: every time another vehicle got between us, I thought I'd lost him. He moved with seeming aimlessness through the side streets of Islington, almost as if he were on a slow motion joy ride. But when we reached the Caledonian Road tube, he stopped so abruptly that I was forced to pass him. I looked in my side window to see that he'd restarted his car, turned the corner and parked. As I waited at a zebra crossing, he got out and moved towards the tube. I hit the accelerator, sped round, parked, jumped out, and almost in the same movement, followed him inside.

I was breathing heavily when I arrived just in time to see his back disappearing into the lift. I shook my head at the ticket collector, who was delaying the gates for me. As soon as he'd pulled the heavy iron doors closed, I took a deep breath and headed for the stairs. I started enthusiastically, leaping down two steps at a time. About half-way down, dizziness caused by the acute bends was forcing me to slow up. At one point, I thought I understood what Tina Schoenberg had meant by a red-out. I turned the final bend, sure that David must be long gone.

I reckoned without the tube repairs. When I reached the platform, it was packed with a crowd of agitated people. Weary day trippers mingled with grouching children while a uniformed BR employee patrolled the length of the platform, promising the imminent arrival of the delayed train.

David had disappeared in the crush, and I stood on tiptoe trying to spot him. When that didn't work, I began to push forward, getting hostile looks but little comment from the strangers I touched on my way. Before I knew it, I was in the front line, the crowd jostling behind me. In the distance I could see him standing beside the track. He wasn't alone. His head bent, he was listening to a thick-set man talking agitatedly beside him. Both men kept glancing over their shoulders.

It was then that the crowd inched forwards. From deep inside the tunnel came the sound of an approaching train. I was pushed, slowly but inevitably, towards the electrified rails. I tried to force my way backwards. But there was no resisting the pressure. As the train shot into sight a hand grasped my shoulder.

'We can't have an accident,' a smooth voice muttered in my ear.

The scream that came from deep inside me was echoed along the platform. Long after I'd stopped, a woman carried on. The squeal of the tube's breaks turned the platform into a nightmare. From the back, people impatient at the delay were pushing forwards. Against them the front ranks were edging away from the horror below them. I looked towards the site of the confusion. David Munger was no longer there. My gaze locked onto David's companion. He had been looking at the track but now he straightened up and calmly scanned the crowd.

Only then did I realise what had happened. The man was acting too cool. His gaze was measured; his calm, calculated. My body winced at the horror of it, as I stepped back to avoid his eyes. Here was a man who had just killed David Munger and he was looking round to see if anybody had spotted him do it.

Reassured, he began to push his way through the crowd. Nobody took much notice of him. What had started with panic had been converted to confusion, and the arrival of various officials and the shaken train driver did little to calm things down. I followed the man. He was a pro. I've never seen anybody walk so expertly through a crowd; it almost parted in front of him. He reached the lift just as it was unloading another bunch of passengers. I was near enough to see him hurry towards the lift operator, mumble something and pass him money. They both stepped back into the empty lifts and the doors closed.

I ran for the stairs. I knew I'd never get to the top in time, but I felt that I had to keep moving. The shock made me unwilling to slow down and think about what I'd seen. The climb seemed easy and even when I got to the top, I didn't register how tired

I was. Instead I looked around and then rushed towards the entrance.

My way was blocked by the ticket collector.

'Tickets please,' he said.

'I haven't got one and I haven't been anywhere. Please let me pass — I'll explain later.'

I was out of luck. I often use Caledonian Road tube and I frequently chat with four out of the five ticket collectors who work the shifts. The fifth one did have to be on duty. His whole demeanour and his pinched face proclaimed that he wasn't going to do anyone any favours. He gripped my arm and with his other hand smoothed his cap over his lank brown hair.

'I expect you know that it's an offence to travel on the underground without a valid ticket and with intention to defraud London Transport. I must asked you ... '

I closed my ears to the rest. Scrabbling into my purse I extracted some coins which I thrust into his empty hand.

'That won't get you past me,' he said. 'Which station did you board?'

This was getting too much. I jerked my arm away from his and tried to push past. All I achieved was that the man in the pay box got up and made as if to come and protect his colleague. He never made it. Instead he stopped to answer an internal phone.

'Let me go,' I almost screamed at him. 'And don't try acting so righteous with me. I saw you take that money from the man, which must be against regulations. Somebody's been killed on the platform, and the murderer just bribed you to get away.'

A grim smile flitted across his face.

'How you people think I'll be fooled by all this nonsense, I don't understand. You scroungers are all the same. Plenty of imagination but you don't like it when you get caught, do you? Come along now.'

He was twisting my arm back when the other man shot out of the ticket office.

'What's going on here?' he shouted. 'Let her go. Somebody's fallen on the track downstairs and all hell's broke loose. They want to know what the lift's doing up here empty.'

I stayed just long enough to get the satisfaction of seeing the

112

ticket collector blanch. He stepped back a pace and shook himself as if to banish me from his sight. Without a word, he hustled the other man into the waiting lift and closed the door.

I knew it was futile, and yet I rushed outside and searched in every direction. Predictably, the man had gone — and all I saw was sparse bank holiday streets.

I didn't realise it, but I was on the point of collapse. All I registered was a glancing sense of relief that the man's disappearance meant I didn't have to confront him. I knew I needed to rest, so I made my way over to Cardozo Road. It seemed to take an awful long time. The lamp posts, my only guide to distance, stretched out distortingly. As I pushed myself along, the face of an old woman curved into focus. 'Getting better at least,' she said and then ducked out of vision.

By the time Anna opened the door, my face was heading for my feet.

She needed only one look. 'What's happened?'

I was too busy holding off the shock to speak. I allowed Anna to lead me in and sit me down. I sat silent, gripping a glass of something that she pressed into my hand. Daniel had appeared, and the two of them sat on either side of me, waiting.

'What is it?' Anna asked.

I told them, or at least I tried. Halfway through, the tears unexpectedly started down my face, and I had to wait until they decided to stop. It didn't feel possible to control them. But gradually I managed to gulp in some calm and to finish the story.

It left me speechless. It didn't do much more for them. We tried to make some sense of it, to work out why my prime suspect had been murdered, but nothing fitted together. Almost, but not quite.

We carried on the discussion over one of Daniel's elegantly presented meals of lemon sole, spinach and fried potatoes. By the end of the meal, the scene in the tube had become less sharp in my mind. It was time to face the police.

Almost two hours had passed since the murder, but the police station was still in uproar. All witnesses had been pulled out of the tube and made to wait in line for interviews. The complaints of bystanders anxious to go home competed with routine questions about names, addresses and occupations. We stood behind an angry old lady who, at regular intervals, called loudly for a chair. Nobody took much notice.

'Next?' The policeman behind the desk didn't bother to glance up.

'I saw what happened,' I said.

He sighed. 'Oh yeah, you and a thousand others. Name?'

'Baeier,' I said and spelt it slowly.

'Okay, how do you spell that?'

Anna gripped my hand. For the next ten minutes the desk man managed to create a new record for the slowest possible collection of details.

'That will be all,' he said when he'd finished. 'We'll be in touch. Next?'

I stood firm against the pressure of the man behind me, who was attempting to get shot of the experience and go home.

'Hold it a minute. I saw the man who did it,' I said.

The policeman looked up, his expression totally blank.

'Did what?' he asked.

'Killed the man on the platform.'

'Look, lady, what makes you assume that the man was killed?'

'Because I saw the man who did it,' I said loudly.

The policeman levered his bulk out of the chair. 'Okay, take a seat, and I'll get somebody to see you,' he sighed.

We squeezed ourselves onto a bench by the wall and waited until another uniformed policeman came out of a side door and called my name. The three of us got up and walked to him.

'Would you come this way, please,' he said, enfolding me in his gesture at the same time as he pushed Anna and Daniel back. 'Your friends can wait here.'

I resisted his propulsion. 'I'd rather they came with me.'

'Is either of these persons a qualified solicitor?' he asked.

'Why does she need one? She's giving information voluntarily, you know,' Anna said.

'Then she doesn't need protection,' he said, trying to face her down.

She raised her voice. 'You can't do this. If you won't let us in, we will get a solicitor.'

'Well, I suppose it's all right,' he said. 'Come with me.' And he pointed the way to a small dingy, interview room.

We had a long wait. The door was left half-open, and we spent our time trying to overhear the various conversations that passed our way. Eventually the door to the room was pulled wide open, and a young, cocky-looking plainclothes man, equipped with clipboard and policewoman, stepped in.

'Miss Baeier?' he said, sitting down, while his colleagues arranged herself watchfully against the wall. 'Perhaps you could tell me what you saw, and then we'll have the statement typed up for you to sign.'

I gave him a description of everything that had happened on the platform. I left out the bits connecting me to David Munger. When I'd finished, the policeman stood up.

'That's very interesting. Somebody else did think that the man was pushed, but since she was standing directly next to him she's rather hysterical.' He stopped himself from adding, 'and so, definitely untrustworthy.' Apparently people who reacted badly to seeing somebody killed in front of their eyes were not to be taken seriously.

Picking up his notepad, he left the room. We paced it for twenty minutes and during that time failed completely to get one word out of the statue by the wall.

The policeman came back. 'Miss Baeier,' he said.

'Congratulations, that's twice in a row you got it right.'

'You live in Dalston?'

'That's right. I've already given all my details to the man at the desk.'

'I understand you reported a corpse in your flat just four days ago.'

We looked at each other: full marks to the police computer.

'Yes, I did report it. In fact, now I know that the man was only knocked out. I explained everything to the Dalston police at the time.'

'I'm sure you did. That will be all. Sergeant Cotts will show you out,' he said, his hand on the door knob.

Daniel leapt forward. 'Wait a minute, what about the ticket inspector?'

'He's denied all knowledge of the incident. That will be all, thank you.'

'So you're saying Kate's lying,' Daniel persisted.

He glanced my way briefly. 'I wouldn't go as far as that. Witnesses are often unreliable in times of stress. And this lady,' he lowered his voice, 'does have a certain reputation.'

He left the room. Sergeant Cotts seemed glad to have something to do at last as she propelled us towards the entrance with unnatural vigour.

Back at Cardozo Road, my adrenalin left me, and with it all my energy. The two of them tried a bit of conversation but gave up when my face stayed rigid, my mouth closed. A heaviness had descended on me, probably a sort of delayed shock. All I could think about was sleep and I got myself onto the sofa, registered enough to thank Anna for the blanket she placed over me, and passed out.

I woke up at four, not so much refreshed as calm.

'Perhaps you should cancel Michael,' Anna said.

'It's all right, I feel better now. Michael won't affect me anymore than seeing David Munger killed. I'd rather see it through.'

Anna looked as though she had her doubts but kept them to herself.

'I rang Sam up and told him about it,' was all she said.

I nodded and drank the cappuccino that Daniel placed in front of me. I followed it up with a short whisky, which seeped into my blood and finished the work that the sleep had started. As far as I could tell, by the time I reached Sam's flat I was integrated once more.

It was 4.45 when I opened the door, but Michael was early. He and Sam were seated opposite each other, making polite conversation. Neither of them looked easy about it, and I remembered that the two had never got on. I suppose it was a case of different styles and different histories. Sam threw me a glance but didn't say anything. I gathered that he hadn't told Michael about David Munger's death. I didn't either.

Michael gave me a brief smile. It didn't mean anything. He was his usual neat, semi-fashionable self with his straight jeans and light blue airtex shirt, but there was an air of distraction and worry on his face. His blue eyes looked shifty; his wide brow was wrinkled, and I watched him uncrease it with effort.

'It's important that I talk to you, Kate,' he said. 'I think you may be getting out of your depth.'

I nodded and waited for more. He straightened his spine and tried another smile. It was no more successful than the first.

'It is dangerous to meddle with spies,' he said. 'Whatever their origin. They're so frequently talked about in the media, people think they have no sting. We, at AER, know differently. I've come to caution you about proceeding without thought. Leave episonage to the experts.'

'Are you talking about anybody in particular?' I asked.

'David Munger,' he said. 'Aldwyn mentioned that you'd come across his name. David Munger is in some danger … '

David Munger is dead, I thought. But again I didn't say it.

' … and you might further threaten his position if you pry too deeply. Take it from me, David Munger is not relevant to Tim's death. It's an entirely different matter.'

'So why did David try and warn me off? Pretend to be dead in my flat and steal my alto?'

'He wasn't pretending,' Michael said. 'The South Africans knocked him out. He told me all about it. He'd gone to warn you about the dangers, and was followed and assaulted. He took your saxophone as a warning to you. I admit it was a juvenile action but hardly too serious, don't you think?'

'That's not how I see it,' I said.

'What I mean, Kate, is that it's not a question of life and death. And that is what we might be dealing with. After all, Tim was killed.' Michael's voice dropped as he finished the sentence. His eyes filled with water, his posture slumped. I didn't say anything.

After a decent pause, he got up.

'I just thought it my duty to warn you,' he said.

He left a silence behind him. I sat where I was, deep in thought. Gradually the sound of tapping impinged on my consciousness. I looked up. Sam was sitting opposite, his index finger moving rhythmically on the side of his chair. He caught my gaze and stopped. I went back to my reverie. I got a fraction more peace before the tapping started again.

'Okay,' I said. 'I get the message. You want to say something.'

Sam looked embarrassed. He pushed a curl of gray off his forehead and cleared his throat.

'What are you going to do?' he asked.

'Carry on,' I said. 'I've got a few thoughts and I don't like them. I can't leave the whole business hanging.'

'But what if he's right?' Sam said.

'Who? Michael? It's no news to me that this is dangerous. I've just seen David Munger killed.'

'I don't like to say this … ' Sam said. I thought I could guess what was coming. I willed him to stop but he didn't seem to notice.

'I'm worried,' he said. 'If Michael is right, you may be getting yourself in a lot of trouble. Maybe this is the time to leave the investigation to … '

'Who?' I shouted. 'The boys? Is that what you and Michael were talking about before I came in? Arranging my exit because of danger?'

My rage, I knew, had erupted from a long history of so-called protection which always seemed to mean exclusion. In my mind's eye I saw Michael and Sam talking as I entered. What I'd taken for discomfort had been conspiracy: men yet again arranging my life.

I was too furious to stay. I left the flat, slamming the door behind me. On the way out I bumped into Sam's downstairs neighbour who was starting her ritual complaint about noise. She didn't stand a chance. I pushed past and drove to my flat.

Once there, I switched on the answerphone and the television. Four hours of mindless watching before I fell asleep. Eight hours of dreamless sleep.

11.

Tuesday I woke and unclamped my jaw. I made myself some coffee, wandered into the study to gaze at the still unmended window, and then switched on the answerphone. Sam's voice was on it: apologising for his behaviour. I gave him a ring and we spent a sticky phone call trying to clear it up. By the end I'd almost forgiven him: forgiven but not forgotten, I thought.

I got dressed and left the house after planning a route to International News Limited's Fleet Street offices. I had reckoned without the one-ways and soon got trapped into a diversion behind a jack-knifed lorry. It was 11.30 when I arrived. I was just in time to witness the vanguard of crumpled-looking journalists heading single-mindedly for the pub. I sat on a bench and watched the procession. After a while it got all too dispirited, the passing jokes too hackneyed, so I went in search of INL's public entrance.

I walked into a narrow hallway and followed hand-drawn arrows up the three flights of stairs. The building verged towards the seedy, and as I climbed I tried to work out exactly when all the glamour had gone out of journalism. I hadn't gone far into the problem by the time I arrived at a tarnished silver plaque which identified International News Limited's central offices.

I pushed the glass-fronted double doors and stepped into the inquiries section. The room was windowless. I found myself facing a high wooden counter which ran the length of the room, with door at either end. I looked around. All the signs pointed to this being a serious newspaper concern. The walls were lined with racks which were crammed with newsprint. Only two run-down plastic chairs broke the monotony. Behind the counter with her back to the entrance sat a woman who seemed to be simultaneously typing and talking over the phone in French.

As I walked closer, the woman finished her conversation and, swivelling her chair round to face me, smiled engagingly. For a moment I was dumbfounded, since the sounds of typing continued, but then I noticed that, directly behind the receptionist, sat the bent back of a man who was banging two fingers on an old manual Olympia.

The woman smiled again. 'They're over there by the wastebin,' she said in a broad Australian accent.

'Hope they like it there,' I said. 'What are they?'

The typist swore as he hit a wrong key. He tore the paper from the typewriter and, crumpling it up into a tight ball, threw it across the floor.

'Sorry, I was waiting for a messenger service and I thought it

119

was you. I'm only a temp, and things can get confused,' the receptionist giggled unconcerned and gazed at me inquiringly.

'I'd like some information,' I started.

'Well, as far as I understand, and you know I've only been here for two weeks, that's exactly what they deal in. Tell me what you want and I'll put you in touch with the boss,' she jerked her head contemptuously backwards ' ... or that whizz kid over there if you prefer,' she finished softly.

'I'm inquiring about a man called David Munger,' I said.

The typist's reaction was dramatic. One mention of Munger's name worked wonders. He turned round and stared at me. Without uttering a word, he got up, wrenched the right-hand door open and disappeared. The receptionist had followed his movement with surprise. She turned and shrugged nonchalantly.

'That means he's seeing to you. You made him jump all right.' she said, before the interest left her face and she lowered her head in concentration.

I wandered across the room and tried to get comfortable on one of the plastic objects. It wasn't easy.

After ten minutes, I was feeling restless. International News subscribed to a comprehensive number of newspapers, but I didn't feel like newsprint. I shuffled along the room trying to occupy myself and eventually ended up in front of the receptionist. She was engrossed, and when I leaned over I noticed she was one clue away from completing the *Guardian* crossword.

'I never can do those things,' I said in admiration.

She looked up. 'You have to keep at them, and they get easier. In this place the time stretches ahead, so I have to do something or I'd go insane.'

'Why, isn't there much work?' I asked.

'How would I know? The creep who just walked out spends his whole day making sure I don't look at anything. All I get to do is answer the phone and talk the occasional phrase of French. I don't know why they hired me. I'm a glorified status-symbol-cum-tea-maker.'

'Do you always temp?'

She put her crossword aside and settled back. The artificial lighting gave everything in the room a harsh edge, but I noticed that close up she looked good. Slightly sunburned, with smooth skin and well-cut brown hair framing her round face, she gave off a healthy glow. She didn't look the type to stay in these surroundings very long.

'Yeah, I always temp. Permanent secretarial work's a mug's game. I do as little as I can get away with, work six months and travel the rest. I'm just on my way to India, but my boyfriend got held up coming to meet me, so I'm earning a bit more. This office is a real drag: I'll be out soon.'

As she talked, the left-hand door opened and two men came out to stand behind her. For the first time I saw the typist's full face. He had all the symptoms of a hack: his tie slightly askew, his top button undone and shirt sleeves untidily rolled, with a pointed anxious face. The other man seemed surer of himself. Wearing a smart gray suit with bland tie to match, he was a big man with red in his complexion and too many rich lunches under his belt.

'What can I do to help you?' he asked. His Afrikaaner voice contained a quality of menace in it which was heightened by the way both men were pushing their chests towards the counter. The smaller man looked ridiculous in his bravado, but the older one could scare me without much effort. He carried his body like a man who used it as a weapon.

I took a deep breath, praying that my voice wouldn't quaver. I was in luck.

'I'm inquiring about a man called David Munger,' I said. 'I understand that he worked for you.'

'Who told you that?' the back-up man asked, a studied sneer on his face.

I didn't say anything. I waited. The big man took his time, scrutinising me. When he was satisfied he drew himself up and gave me the full force of this size.

'Mr Munger is no longer with us,' he said, and wheeled round.

'Does that mean with International News or with this world?' I called as his number two turned to follow him.

They both froze — the small type saving himself just in time from catapulting into the other's back. Then they presented their faces again.

'Look, Miss ... ?' the big man said briskly, as I just stood there,

' … whoever you are. We run a tight office here and we are all working to deadline. I would appreciate it if you would leave my staff to continue without further interruption.'

His staff responded variously. While the receptionist made no attempt to hide her amazement at the proceedings, the journalist went into an intensely busy and tough act. Standing on my dignity, I moved out slowly.

I ran fast down the stairs. Before I registered that I'd hit the pavement, I was squinting into the sun's glare. I walked a few paces down the block and then stopped myself. The International News chief didn't look the kind to miss out on his lunch, so I decided to hang around in case he took his side-kick with him. I had the feeling that if I could get the receptionist alone, she'd be only too pleased to help. I'd learnt from my back-breaking typing days that that's the one sure thing about temps — they have no developed sense of loyalty or responsibility to their bosses. I reckoned it was worth a try and I strolled round, looking for camouflage.

I rapidly came to the conclusion that I had a lot to learn before I'd qualify as an urban guerrilla. I settled for the window of the stationer's shop which was cited opposite the INL entrance.

I learned a lot about ballpoints and, at one point, became so engrossed in doing a consumer comparison that I almost forgot to watch out for the reflections of the two men. I thought I'd missed them, but at 12.30 the INL door opened and they emerged, deep in conversation. I stood tight until they'd disappeared into a pub and then I sprinted back to their offices.

The receptionist hadn't moved, except to place a brown-bread sandwich and a rosy apple in front of her. She looked up at me without a trace of surprise.

'You're back. I suppose you know they've gone to lunch. I never take a lunch break. I get paid by the hour, so if I stay here the jerks don't know any better and pay me more.'

I felt uncomfortable. 'I've lost my newspaper. I think I left it here,' I said.

She looked up again and giggled. I liked her for the way she made absolutely no pretence at believing me.

'You're welcome to look,' she said. 'Take your pick. This place is jam-packed with newspapers, and I won't miss one. You rattled those two, all right, didn't you?'

'You're right, I didn't even come in with a newspaper. I came to see if you've got any idea why your bosses acted so aggressively towards me?'

'They went overboard, didn't they? I tell you, in this sort of job, you expect to get treated like a piece of blotting paper — paid to absorb instructions — but those two beat everything. You threw a snake into the pit. After you left, they got me working on the switchboard like there was a fire.'

'Did they say anything interesting?' I asked.

She looked at me before unwrapping her sandwich from its cellophane straitjacket and taking a healthy bite.

'What the hell, I'm leaving the job soon and everybody with their head in the right place knows telephonists listen to the calls — if they're not too boring. They put in a call to the South African Embassy. The conversation featured a woman investigating — that's you, I guess — and David. The embassy told them to calm down and you couldn't do anything.' She finished her sandwich and set to polishing the apple.

'Did you hear what happened to David?' I said.

She took a crunch before she spoke. 'He's dead. He fell off a train. I'm sorry about it — he wasn't such great shakes but compared to the two of them ... Also he kept me in good supplies.'

I smiled understandingly and looked more closely. Gradually it had dawned on me what gave this woman her eerie, slow relaxed quality. The way she ate, savouring each mouthful at the same time as she chewed methodically, reinforced this. The woman was stoned. She was hanging around until India, biding her time with enough grass to take the edge off the monotony.

'What would it be like if I took a quick look around their offices?' I asked.

'As far as I'm concerned, very uninteresting. But everyone to her own thing. Go ahead.' She leaned forward and opened a gate which was concealed in the barrier.

'Hold on a minute and I'll stand by the door and keep an eye open. I'll give you a yell if anybody comes,' she said.

I thanked her as we swapped places.

In the twenty minutes it took me to search the offices, I made

123

two discoveries. The first is that there's more to searching an office than meets the eye; and the second, that, whatever the skill involved, I just don't have the nerve. I spent the entire time feeling like I was about to be stabbed in the back or expecting the heavy tap on the shoulder. And this despite the fact that Michelle, the receptionist, kept up a continual stream of reassuring chatter.

Behind the counter was easy: apart from the manual typewriter and one dead-looking golfball, there was only an in-tray filled with miscellaneous articles and an out-tray of gray envelopes. Michelle offered to fill me in on all their contents, but I didn't take her up on it. Instead I walked into the room on the right.

If the newsprint scene outside had been intense, then this room was in a wholly different league. It was the library, and box files which were stacked to the ceiling competed for space with the filing cabinets, all of which, except the last, were locked. And that one was empty. The room, Michelle informed me, was the one in which David had worked. He'd done some sort of writing and liaison work there.

By the time that I moved into the second room, my anxiety level was high. It was the big man's office with its executive-type desk and two comfortable swivel chairs. The man was a neat worker. Everything was placed in little piles and three sharpened pencils smartly demarcated the ends of the working area.

I walked to his comfortably upholstered chair, sat down and opened the drawers. They were crammed. There was no way I would have time to go through all the material so neatly filed in them.

I glanced along the titles. No obvious labels like 'Murder' or 'Spies' sprang to the eye, so I picked 'Finances'. Inside the snazzy plastic folder was an extensive correspondence on smooth, white paper — all straight and placed in chronological order. It was a pleasure to see, but all I got out of the file was the other party to the correspondence — the Organisation of Information Services.

From behind the door, Michelle called out cheerfully. Fright almost catapulted me into the dustbin. 'How you doing? I'd advise you to stop soon, because they sometimes go out for only half an hour.'

This woman was so relaxed that if she advised me to stop, it was good enough for me. I grabbed another file. This one was headed 'Contracts — miscellaneous'. At least I could check if Tim's name was there.

I ran my eyes down the columns which made up the list. It came as quite a surprise. Tim's name was there all right, with a slight pencil cross besides it, but so were many others. The list read like a *Who's Who* among independent and established journalists in Britain. A few days ago, I'd never heard of INL. But, by the look of this list, they spread themselves around. Before my anxiety got the better of me, I noticed that Miranda Johnson's name was amongst the many.

I put the paper back into the file, the whole lot into the drawer, closed it and stood back a bit to make sure that the pencils were properly regimented and the desk looked unruffled. I edged out, shutting the door and sprinting over the counter. Only when I finally made it to the outer office, did I feel even relatively safe. I thanked Michelle, wished her luck in India, and took the stairs two at a time.

I was a block and a half away before I slowed down. The anxiety had left me empty and hungry. I was just passing Grains, the wholefood restaurant, so I walked in. And as usual, as soon as I sat down with my tray, I regretted it. The atmosphere of the place is fine: nicely laid-out pine tables, comfortable benches and good lighting. The trouble is the food: where tastes blend into one unsatisfying mulch. It all looks good but comes as a big disappointment when it hits the mouth. But I wasn't at my most discriminating and, with my blood sugar levels hitting an all time low, I ate my way through a concoction of pulses and vegetables and drank down the watery lemon vebena tea. After that, I got up, nodded sympathetically to a curly-haired man who was toying dispiritedly with his food, and left.

I found a telephone box quite easily. I had less success with my calls. Nobody answered at African Economic Reports and Diana Nicholson's assistant told me she was at the office. I took the address and made my way to it.

She worked at an interior decorators somewhere at the back of Covent Garden. The outside of the building was pleasant. The interior verged on the overblown. Tubular steel and polished glass fought for attention amongst the plants that would have been more at home in the tropics.

The receptionist tried to get rid of me, but she wasn't in luck. Just as I was beginning to argue, Diana walked into the open-plan entrance hall. With distaste, she gestured me into a small area which was encased by glass and looked like it would keel over if somebody introduced a curve into it. I lowered myself into a geometric item which was scarcely more comfortable than it appeared.

'I've got an apology for you,' I said.

Diana took out a cigarette, produced an elegant silver holder, and joined the two together. She didn't bother to light the result.

'I believe you about David Munger,' I said. 'You didn't know him.'

'I have no need for your visits ... or for your approval,' she said. 'I know when I speak the truth. Even if everybody chooses to doubt my word.'

'Did Tim make the same accusations?' I said.

She reached under her desk and withdrew a rectangular object, bright red and smooth. She pressed a concealed catch at the bottom and held the flame to her cigarette. She was doing her best to act self-assured, but she forgot to draw in. The cigarette went out.

'What is going on between Robert Slick and you?' I said. 'What are you both hiding?'

'Why on earth would I want to tell you?' she asked. It was meant to sound tough, but it sounded like a plea.

'It might relieve your mind. It can't be that bad. Why don't you try me. Is it something to do with Tim's mother?' I said.

Diana was thinking and she showed it. Two furrows made dents between her flawless eyebrows.

'What is your attitude to the police?' she said.

I looked at her inquiringly.

'I mean, would you go to them with information that might be seen as relevant, but isn't?' she asked.

'Not if it wasn't relevant,' I said.

Her head relaxed, the furrows disappeared and she leaned across the desk.

'Robert Slick once had an affair with Tim's mother,' she said. 'There was talk that Tim was Robert's son. I've never known the truth of it. I don't think Tim did either.'

126

I nodded, wondering where all this was leading.

'It caused a scandal at the time,' she continued. 'Tim's father heard about it and divorced Mrs Nicholson. They were never happy anyway and he used it as an excuse. But Robert rejected Mrs Nicholson, told Tim's father that he'd been led astray, and the two men remained friends. It was Robert who helped Tim's father draw up a will that would exclude Mrs Nicholson from getting any money. Robert is a very upright man and I think he thought she'd started the scandal to ruin him.'

'And twenty-five years later?' I prompted.

'Twenty-five years later, Tim decided to rewrite his will. He didn't want to leave the money to me — I didn't see why he should — but instead to organisations he was politically interested in. Robert Slick was distressed. I think because he'd regarded Tim as his son, and now Tim was going to leave his money to everything that Robert stood against.'

'So Robert stopped him,' I said.

Diana looked straight at me. She seemed to be asking for something but I couldn't guess what. She dropped her head.

'I don't know,' she said. 'I'm so confused. I can no longer tell.'

'What happened the night you went to Tim's office?' I asked. 'Maybe I can work it out.'

'We had an argument,' she said. 'Tim started in on me about David Munger. I didn't know what he was talking about. He called me a liar. He said I was immoral and decadent. Then he threw the old will at me. Told me I wasn't going to get a penny. He said he was going to sign a new one as soon as I'd gone. I tried to make him believe that the money wasn't important, but he didn't want to know. He kept taunting me about it. In the end I left.'

'And sent me the will after I'd come to see you?'

'Yes,' she said. 'It didn't seem right to keep it. I thought that it would get you out of my hair. Robert didn't like it.'

'How did he get into the story?' I asked.

'I told him about it. He advised me to keep quiet, not to tell the police I'd been there. He said it would look suspicious for me.'

'What happened to the new will?' I said. 'Did you see it?'

'I ... I took it away,' she said. 'I was so angry I grabbed it from his hands and left. I would have given it back but then, when I heard about his death, I panicked and I ... I burnt it. It wasn't signed. He didn't have time for that. So it wouldn't have made any difference, would it?'

I let the question lie and got up to go. Just before I was out of the glass model, I turned to her.

'Why are you telling me all this?' I said.

'Because you'll find it out sooner or later,' she said. 'From the person in the office.'

'What person?' I asked.

'There was somebody there the whole time, who must have heard. I knew there was somebody when Tim wouldn't let me in through the door. He was always embarrassed about my existence. He tried to keep his history, his past mistakes,' and she smiled wryly, 'from the rest of you.'

I nodded and opened the door. Her voice followed me out.

'I shan't keep the money,' she said. 'It's tainted for me.'

12.

Ron lived in a communal house on the edge of Highbury. Because of the number of surrounding council houses, it was an area which had still not felt the incursion of the migrating middle classes. Only the occasional 'for sale' notice showed that things were changing. For the most part, the street exuded an air of gentle decay.

His house was on the corner, surrounded by a generous garden. As I walked up the path, I saw the rows of sprouting lettuces which threatened to encroach onto the weed-covered flower beds. I took the brass knocker in my hands and let it fall. A fleck of paint came with it. I heard a scuffle from within, and then Rhoda opened the door.

'Hi,' I said. 'I haven't congratulated you yet.'

She was in the full flush of pregnancy, if not of health. Her dark curly hair had lost some of its bounce and the remains of her New York twang sounded flatter than ever. She grimaced.

'I spend most of the time over the toilet bowl,' she said. 'I feel more like I'm going to seed than pregnant.'

'Leave it to your lettuces. Going to seed, that is,' I said.

'Yeah, they're pathetic aren't they? A relic. We're not allowed to eat them after the latest GLC lead scare. Would you like some tea or have you joined the ranks of the tannin haters?'

'No, I haven't,' I said. 'I just don't like tea at all. Is Ron in?'

'He's upstairs in his room with his sticking. On the first landing.'

It was a house set on many levels. On my first go, I missed the landing. I retraced my steps and knocked on a purple door whose lack of any handle explained why I'd taken it for an airing cupboard. When nobody answered, I pushed the door open and walked in. I didn't get far.

'Don't move,' he shouted.

Ron was hunched in the middle of the floor, his back to the door. He was surrounded by what looked like slivers of plastic, with the occasional matchstick interspersed amongst them. It took me a while to work it out. In front of him was a half-finished construction — an intricate miniature ocean liner. Rhoda's description had been apt. Ron was definitely sticking.

I gave the room the once over. It's conflicting images confused me. The double bed, typewriter and solid block of books above the desk all proclaimed the professional journalist, but they were mere trimmings. The rest was adolescent. The walls were plastered with pictures of boats and fancy-looking plans. Dotted around at eye level were glass cages which enclosed models. Each was neatly finished and neatly labelled, a monument to hours of precise work.

My eyes returned to Ron. I found him looking at me inquiringly.

'I can move?' I said.

'Now you can. I'd lost number 521 and was terrified I'd never find it again,' he said. He held up a piece of something shapeless and synthetic.

'What is this?' I said. 'Construction by numbers?'

Ron looked hurt. It suited his open face. 'It's my hobby,' he said. 'Did you want something special?'

'I tried to phone you at work,' I said. 'Nobody was in.'

The hurt changed to embarrassment. He distracted my attention from the red on his face by removing his gold-rimmed glasses and holding them up to the light.

'We thought it was a good time to have some distance,' he said. He didn't sound convinced.

'You boys not getting on too well?' I asked.

I wished I hadn't. His face closed up. Emotion left it, and with it went the blush.

'What do you want, Kate?' he said.

'Information,' I answered. 'Something that will lead me to Tim's killer.'

'Why do you assume he was killed?' he asked.

'Two reasons really,' I said. 'Number one, you hired me to assume that; and, number two, David Munger is dead. He was killed.'

Ron blinked once. There was a pause, and then he blinked again. It was like he was trying to shut out the news. He moved from the bed where he'd been sitting and into the middle of the room. He stared at the half-finished model. He leaned down and examined it closely. He was making up his mind about something.

'I liked Tim,' was what he came up with.

'Unlike Aldwyn,' I said.

'The two of them never got on. Tim was trying to run away from his background and thought that Aldwyn was moving towards what he'd rejected. That stung Aldwyn's pride. But you expect tensions like that when you work with people. It's part of life. Tim knew that, even if he did go overboard towards the end.'

'Like how?'

'He started making accusations. He got carried away. He insinuated something about spies.'

'Did he say David Munger was a spy?' I said.

'David Munger, yes. But that wasn't only it. He accused Michael of being one.'

'And you didn't believe him?'

Ron picked up the model and twisted it round. A piece came off. He shoved it into the pockets of his canvas trousers and looked defiantly at me.

'No,' he said. 'I didn't. Would you?'

'Not really. It's an easy accusation in your line of work, but I can't see what would be in it for Michael. He'd lose everything he values and gain nothing.'

'That's what I thought,' Ron said. 'Even if ... '

He left it trailing there.

'Even if Aldwyn did take it more seriously for a while,' he said. 'Of course that didn't last long, but it caused a lot of disruption on the way. We have to trust each other. We have to trust each other.'

He said quickly and with desperation. Something was sticking in his conscience.

'What are you hiding, Ron?' I asked.

He stood in the middle of the floor looking lost. His ears, protruding from his chaotic brown hair, gave him an almost comical appearance.

'Nothing,' he said. 'Exactly nothing.'

There was an air of decision in his voice. I stuck my hand in the gap between the door and its post and pulled it open. Ron was still standing motionless when I left.

Sam was there when I arrived at his flat. He got up when I came in and made a move towards me. He stopped himself before he reached me.

'Still angry?' he said.

'Marginally. Just don't do it again. I've just about had my fill of men and their manoeuvres.'

I was interrupted by the phone. It was for me. I picked it up to hear a deep voice on the other end. He said his name was Joseph and we had a mutual friend. I gathered he was talking about Zoe.

'We have examined your information,' he said. 'It has proved quite interesting. Do we have your permission to use it?'

'If it helps,' I said. 'Although it's not mine. I'd be grateful if you got in touch with people at African Economic Reports before you do. Tim Nicholson put it together.'

'Of course we will co-operate with them,' he said. 'There is another matter. Our friend says you were interested in a young South African.'

'Yes,' I said.

'Well, so are we. We wondered whether you would go and see his parents. They're flying in tonight. They'll be staying at the Berkeley in Kensington.'

'See them about what?' I said.

'Background information. Anything you can find out about the man in question.'

I agreed to do it. Joseph said he'd be in the office the next day. I said I might drop by.

As soon as the line went dead, I dialled Miranda Johnson's number. It took a long time before she answered. When she did, she didn't sound too excited to hear my voice. I asked her about International News Limited. She got annoyed.

'Already told AER,' she said. 'Have they no filing systems?'

'Who did you tell?' I asked.

'Tim Nicholson. Know he's dead, but really he could have told the others. Said he would investigate.'

'Investigate what?' I asked.

'INL. Something wrong with them. Approached me to write background articles on unions and didn't use anything in any paper I've ever heard of. Don't believe they were really interested at all. Asked a lot of peculiar questions.'

'Like what?' I said.

'Can't remember now. Questions about people I knew … think that was it. Didn't answer. They never did pay me. Peculiar organisation. That's why I told Tim about them. All I know, really.'

13.

By the next morning, I realised how tired I was. Fatigue seeped through my body and invaded my consciousness. I felt like I'd been stuck on the investigation so long that I'd never become unglued.

I thought about phoning the Berkeley and decided against it. Instead I got up, found a skirt that give me an approximation of respectability, and took the tube to Kensington.

The Mungers, the hotel clerk informed me, had arrived the night before and hadn't yet left their room. He offered to give them a call. I said I'd rather surprise them. He didn't seem to care.

I took the velvet-lined lift to the third floor and wafted down the soulless corridors. Their room was on a corner, the last in a long line of anonymous doors.

A woman answered my knock. She was dressed in a mauve silk shirt which sat above a flared skirt, its lines fashioned to make her look thinner. Golden chains lined her neck, a heavy diamond weighed down her left hand. Her face looked drained. Jet lag and grief had done it.

She nodded when I gave her my name. She nodded when I asked if I could talk to her. She nodded when I asked if I could come in. She let me walk past her. She didn't appear to have taken in anything that I'd said.

A man was standing on the balcony when I entered. He turned to face me. He was a tall man, heavily built and solidly padded with muscles that were fated to turn to fat in a few years' time. His clothes accentuated his bulk: a closely fitting gray suit, fitted for tightness but not for discomfort, the trousers ending in short flares. The wide-shouldered jacket enclosed a white shirt and black tie, complete with emblem.

'What do you want?' he asked. His voice filled the room with its anger.

'This young lady knew David,' the woman's voice came from behind me. 'She'd like to ask us a few questions.'

The man shrugged and turned back to his balcony. He stared intently at the two pots of pink geraniums. Their leaves were seamed with yellow as if they were beginning to mutate in the Kensington fumes.

'It must have been a great shock to you,' I said.

The woman nodded. A strand of her yellow hair fell in front of her eye. She made no attempt to dislodge it. The man on the balcony didn't move.

'Had you kept in touch with him?' I asked.

David's mother looked towards her husband. It was a look I didn't envy, a look that was balanced between recrimination and misery. He caught it as he turned round.

'We weren't on speaking terms,' he said. 'The boy couldn't even extend common courtesy to me. That's all I expect in my own house: courtesy. From all the members of my household.'

'You didn't get on?'

David's mother sat on the fake Elizabethan chair that stood in front of a rectangular mirror. She stared into it as if trying to extract the past.

'John isn't David's father,' she explained. 'He's my second husband. They never did get on.'

The man moved into the room. He tried to laugh. It got strangled halfway.

'All I asked was common courtesy,' he muttered. 'And respect for his elders. How could I stand there while he cheeked his mother, came in at all hours, giving us nothing but trouble?'

'Is that why David left South Africa?' I asked.

'Oh, he wasn't thinking of us, I can assure you. Got himself into a hell of jam and found a way out, didn't he? Thought he'd leave the country to breathe, he said, away from our suffocating culture. I could have given him culture,' the man said. His large hand enfolded itself. The knuckles on the fist he made were white.

'That's not fair,' David's mother said. 'He was in trouble.'

The man snorted in derision.

'What sort of trouble?' I asked.

'He was arrested along with a whole group of students. I don't know what they were doing. Probably nothing. I don't like to speak against our police but sometimes they get carried away with their duty. I suppose we do live in difficult times,' she said. 'They kept David in John Voster Square. We went to the top, my husband's practice means he meets people that matter, but we weren't told anything. And then, suddenly, David was released. Just like that. He turned up wearing the same clothes I'd last seen him in.'

'And he left soon after?'

'No, he went away first,' she said.

'Where to?'

'Do you think he bothered to tell us?' the man interrupted. A look from her stilled him.

'We don't know. He told us he was going and we shouldn't worry. He said he was going to learn a few things about reality,' she said.

'How did he seem?' I said.

'A combination,' she said. 'He worried me. He was both

134

triumphant and bitter. Like something was happening that he couldn't control and he'd decided not to care.'

'And what happened when he came back?'

'He wouldn't talk about it. Then he said he wanted to leave the country.'

The man couldn't restrain himself any longer. He went up behind her and put his hands on her shoulders. It could have been comforting. It looked menacing.

'Wanted, hell! Said he'd been told to. Making himself into a big hero. Throwing my service record in my face. Who did he think he was?'

'He was my son,' she said, softly.

His gaze softened. His hands touched her hair. They were in a world of their own. I left, closing the door quietly behind me.

The stairs up to Joseph's office were a peril in themselves. Structurally, they never stood much chance, but they'd been made worse by the accumulation of boxes, all battered, which lined each side. I negotiated my way up them and through a long corridor. Joseph came to a door and gestured me in.

He was dressed in a suit ten years out of date. Baggy brown, with an ill-fitting jacket, it failed to conceal the air of authority he carried around with him. His shirt was frayed at the collar. It didn't seem to matter. I sat on a plastic covered armchair. He sat opposite me, his feet planted apart, his hands resting on two expansive thighs.

I told him about my visit to the Berkeley. He didn't say much, just asked for clarification on several points, and nodded grimly to himself. Then he got up and walked over to a battered-looking filing cabinet. From it, he extracted a cardboard folder which he set on a trestle table that stood by the door. With one swipe he moved the pile of papers that occupied the space and then he opened the folder.

'I'd like you to look at these photographs,' he said.

I got up and went to the table. It was thick file. I flipped through the pictures, wondering what I was doing it for.

They were, almost without exception, pictures of white men.

Men whose background was obvious, their features set into that sort of brutal solidity which masks the thoughts of so many whites in South Africa. All the pictures had been taken in Trafalgar Square. South Africa House made a guest appearance on several of them. I flipped through them one by one. They didn't mean anything to me. Nothing, that is, until I was almost at the end.

'That's him,' I shouted. 'The man who killed David Munger.'

Joseph reached for it and turned it over.

'The Butcher, we call him. Security branch. Was known to have been present at police stations when several of our comrades were tortured. He came over here about six months ago. We suspected he'd come to watch over spies who'd been recruited during interrogation. Now it seems we were right.'

'Why would he kill David Munger?' I asked.

Joseph looked into the distance for along time.

'Your friend Tim Nicholson came to a conclusion we've long suspected,' he said at last. 'A secret agreement between South Africa and Argentina exists ... they plan to make nuclear bombs. When the news gets out, South Africa will be severely embarrassed.'

'But what has that got to do with David?' I asked.

Joseph got up and stood by the window, his back to me. When he turned round his face showed he'd made a decision.

'You may as well know,' he said. 'This won't stay secret for long. David Munger was a Boer spy, in the pay of the apartheid regime.'

'How do you know?' I asked.

'It fits. We're learning to identify them. When Munger first came to England he contacted us. He said he wanted to do work for the movement. He said he'd been arrested carrying literature for one of our people and his arrest had made him want to work against the regime. We almost believed him, but we had reservations. He had been an uncommitted casualty: doing something that should have been safe but had turned wrong because of an unexpected police operation. He'd never independently involved himself while in the country. He even did military service. We used him, but only on the fringes of the organisation. And then we became suspicious.'

'Why?'

'First of all,' Joseph pushed one of his brown stubby fingers into the air, 'he had too much money. It made the comrades wonder. We investigated his job. As you've discovered, he worked for International News Limited, which is funded by the Organisation of Information Services. We had our eyes on them.'

'Are they South African, too?'

'No, it's an English organisation. Small but rich. It has on its board several prominent Conservative MPs who have been known to favour the Boer regime. We thought they've been receiving funds from South Africa, and some of the revelations during Muldergate hinted at this. We think they pass on some of the money to INL which the regime uses as a front to gather information. INL pretends to syndicate news. But none of it is published.'

'That sounds pretty damning for David,' I said.

'That's not all,' another finger punched the air. 'Certain of our people who came to London and who met David Munger here went back and were picked up. The security branch knew too much about them. Little details, not important in themselves. But it showed that somebody had informed on them. We edged David out. Also we kept a watch on him, but we don't have the resources for that sort of thing. Now we know.'

'What happened after you got rid of him?'

'He lay low. We lost sight of him. Then he surfaced. He kept away from us and from South African circles, and instead took up with your friends. We couldn't work out why, until this nuclear story started making sense. He took up with your outfit to get more information about it.'

'Maybe you can't answer this,' I said. 'But what motivated David? Why should he spy?'

Joseph's hand came down to the side of the chair. It made a dull thud.

'It happens,' he said. 'A young white man who considers himself a liberal. He becomes involved without thinking about it and finds himself suddenly in the nightmare of detention. He's got no reason to keep on our side, he has too much to lose, and he breaks. Possibly he wants to blame us for that ... it's his way of justifying his actions. Possibly he wants revenge against those who led him into trouble. It happens. We can never be sure why. And the security police aren't slow to exploit it. Look how they sent him away for training so soon. And then out of the country. He wouldn't have been allowed an independent thought from the moment he first tried to please them.'

My mind was doing spirals. I had to ask him again.

'Why would that lead David to his death?'

'Maybe he had second thoughts. Maybe he thought your friend Tim had been killed by the South Africans. Spies recruited through fear are notoriously unreliable. They pretend to themselves that what they're doing is right. But then something may happen that cracks this image of themselves.'

'Are you saying that Tim was killed by the South Africans?'

Joseph shook his head. He shuffled the photographs into a pile and replaced them in the file. He shook his head again.

'I wouldn't think so,' he said. 'They would lose more than they gained. The British government overlooks a great deal, but it wouldn't like a British subject murdered on its own patch.'

I nodded and got up. We shook hands and then I left. The stairs felt even more perilous on the way down.

I spent the journey back to Sam's flat in thinking hard. I didn't like what I came up with, but I couldn't get rid of it. When I arrived I found three people, Anna, Daniel and Sam, there.

'I've got a problem,' I said. 'I'm glad you're here in fact. I need some help.'

I told them about my visit to David Munger's parents and the later revelations.

'But who killed Tim?' Daniel said.

'That's the problem. I think I know and I don't like it.'

'Who was it?' Daniel said again.

'We all hate the South African police,' I said. 'Right?'

They nodded.

'And we have difficulties with people on the left sometimes?'

Again three nods.

'I think somebody we know killed Tim. Somebody who's fucked up, but somebody who's not the enemy in the sense that a member

138

of the South African security police is.'

'Who?' This time it came from Daniel and Sam simultaneously. I ignored them.

'I don't know what to do about it. The thing is,' I said. 'Does justice have to be done?'

'You know and you're wondering whether to tell the police?' Anna asked.

'Not the police,' I said. How could I do that? I know who killed Tim, but I'm not so sure why. I've got an inkling. But who knows what makes somebody take the step?'

'So are you wondering whether to tell anybody?' Anna said.

'Yes,' I said. 'Does it make any difference now Tim's dead?'

'Maybe a people's court,' Sam said.

'For what? A mock trial to humiliate somebody? What will that do?'

'It's not what that'll do, it's what you'll do,' Sam was leaning forward in his chair, his eyes afire. 'I'm sorry that wasn't very articulate. What I mean is that you can't bear the burden. It's not for you to hold the power in your hands. You were set to investigate something and you've come to the end of it. How can you now suppress your findings?'

'That's like justice,' I said. 'Scientific method: the truth will out. But that's talking in ultimates. This isn't the revolution; just one of those hiccups probably caused by the frustrations of all our lives. Gramsci called them morbid symptoms.'

'Who's talking in clichés now?' Sam asked.

I started to retort but Anna stopped me.

'I think Sam's right,' she said. 'You can't decide. Why not tell us all about it?'

I felt completely stuck inside and so I told them. I gave them my reasons, from the trivial, through the collected clues, to my feelings about the dynamics of AER. They listened in silence. They asked a few questions when I'd finished. After that, we discussed it: played with the possibilities and worked out a strategy. I made some phone calls and then came back into the room and tried to get drunk. I didn't have enough time or inclination.

At last I had to go. I refused offers to accompany me and started for the door. As I was almost out, Anna's voice made me look back.

'I wonder if you, if we, would have felt differently, if it was a woman who had been killed.'

'I wonder,' I said.

14.

I arrived at the Carelton Building in record time. I wished for a slow tube, but I was out of luck. I chose the stairs at Oxford Circus but that took no time at all. I stopped for a moment by some buskers: two women, the one looking like she'd come from a country weekend in the best of her twinsets, the other dressed in tights and a jumper, her bright purple hair sticking up straight on her head. They were playing a piece by Vivaldi on two violins. The piece came to an end, as they all do, and I walked on.

They must have heard me climbing the stairs. My tread was heavy enough. When I opened the door, they all stirred, but their movements were without any meaning.

Ron was seated by Tim's desk, playing with a pile of paper clips. He'd arranged them to make a large question mark. When he saw me glance at the pattern, his hand swept across it. It was an uncontrolled gesture, and a flurry of paper clips hit the ground. He made no attempt to pick them up.

Michael was sitting almost opposite him, his head in his hands. He was massaging his left temple, but any relief he was getting from the pressure must have been ruined by the odd angle of his neck. It was twisted to one side as if he couldn't bear to look towards the door. Instead, his eyes were fixed at a spot on the floor which coincided with Aldwyn's tan sneakers.

They were a neat sight, as was Aldwyn. But the various autumnal shades he sported did little to subdue the impression of pent-up fury that he exuded. His feet stayed still, but the effort showed. I thought I could detect faint tremblings in his legs, and the hands that he held behind his back were busy clutching each other too hard. When he spoke, the strain in his voice belied the bravura of his words.

'I hope you can justify this meeting,' he said. 'I have been pulled away from valuable work at home. And I, for one, would like to say that we desire to finish this business as soon as possible. I think it would be correct to say that I speak for us all.'

I pulled a chair from behind a desk, turned it round and sat down. My hands I kept together, so as to steady them.

'I know who killed Tim,' I said.

I'd half hoped for some sort of response, to make the telling of it easier. I wasn't in luck. Nobody spoke. Nobody moved. I took a deep breath and then began.

'Let's start on the night Tim was killed,' I said.

'Died,' Ron said. He didn't sound convinced.

'Tim was killed,' I said, 'on that Friday night. Let's look at your alibis. You'd all been in the office that day but you all left. Ron says he was in the pub. Aldwyn was with him, but left to talk to Tim about the tension in AER. He says he didn't manage it, because Tim was having an argument with a woman and he didn't want to interfere. She was a woman he'd never seen before. Michael had left earlier but he says he returned to pick up some papers. Michael says Tim was alone and that he left him, alive, in the office.'

'Get on with this charade,' Michael snapped. 'What's the point of reiterating all this?'

'To get to the end,' I said. 'I don't know how else to tell it.'

'Are we now supposed to feel pity for you?' Aldwyn asked.

The dig hit home. For a moment my jaws clamped shut, my mouth refused to move. With an effort, I unfroze.

'That Friday, Tim did have a visitor. It was his ex-wife, Diana Nicholson. Tim and Diana had a furious argument, it was partly about Tim's will, but Diana says that Tim provoked her into it by raising something else. She also says that somebody was in the AER office and heard the whole thing.'

'I cannot understand why you won't shorten this scene, Kate,' Aldwyn said. 'Who did this Diana say she saw?'

'As you yourself confirmed, Diana and Tim were arguing in the hall. Let's leave that for a minute. I think it would be better to discuss the argument. Basically, it started because Tim accused Diana of having an affair with David Munger.'

'He's dead,' Ron said. 'I heard yesterday. He fell in front of a tube.'

'He was pushed,' I said. 'I was there.'

Michael's hand stopped massaging. For the first time, he looked directly at me.

'I warned you,' he said, 'You and Sam. I told you not to meddle in this situation. I told you it was dangerous.'

'You warned me too late,' I said. 'And besides ... '

Michael was on his feet. Rage tightened his lips, whitened his eyes.

'You must have drawn the attention of his enemies to him. Why else was he killed?'

'He was killed because of Tim's death. He believed that the South African regime, his masters, had murdered Tim. He was killed because he was a South African agent who stepped out of line.'

'He was an ex-agent,' Aldwyn said. We've been through this all before.'

'He was an agent,' I said. 'Without the ex. He was interested in AER because of the work Tim was doing. He was trying to find out how much Tim knew about the plans to build a nuclear bomb in co-operation with the Argentinian junta. Tim wasn't the only one he was spying on. David Munger got involved with a woman, her name's Tina Schoenberg, just because she had met Tim and she worked in the Argentine Embassy. David thought Tina had given Tim the information on the bomb. David also looked through Tim's address book, searching for contacts. That's where he got Diana Nicholson's address. Perhaps he was going to try and get to Tim through her. He never got the chance.'

'And perhaps your imagination has taken off without you,' Aldwyn said. 'David Munger came here quite openly. He was helping us with various details.'

'That's not all he was doing,' I said. 'He was also meeting somebody secretly.'

'Why on earth would he do that?' Aldwyn asked.

'I'm not sure why. I think it was just a way of creating conspiratorial atmosphere around him, a climate of intrigue which would help him find out things that might otherwise be kept away from him: a sort of divide and rule tactic.'

When I finished there was silence. I waited for them to ask a question, again to make my life easier. But they didn't. I glanced at Ron. He was using the quiet to bend down and collect the paper clips. His hands were shaking. He tried to make a fist. He failed, and so they scattered through the gaps in his fingers. I resisted the temptation to get up and help him. Instead, I forced myself to continue.

'David Munger was meeting Michael secretly,' I said.

'That's the most ridiculous accusation I have ever heard in my entire life,' Michael said. 'Why would I do that?'

'You tell me,' I said.

He pushed his head up. Sweat made a line across his forehead. He tried to brush it away but he missed. He wasn't concentrating. 'You have no proof,' he said.

'David used to meet you by taking out adverts in *Street Times*. The code would be easy to work out. The only month he missed was April: the month when you were out of the country, on holiday.'

Michael opened his mouth and then shut it. It was Ron who came up with words.

'What has this to do with Tim?' he said. The paper clips hit the floor once more as he straightened his back.

'Tim found out about the meetings. He tested his theories out by placing his own advert. Then he must have followed Michael to Camden Lock. That's where Michael and David used to meet. Tim was seen there, arguing with David. We'll never know what happened for sure, but I guess Tim put two and two together and came up with conspiracy. He decided that Michael and David were both spies.'

'Are you insinuating that Michael is a spy?' Aldwyn said.

'No, I'm not. But I think that Tim did. He thought that his work, and the work of AER was in serious danger. He was half-right, but he went overboard. He wouldn't believe Diana when she said she didn't know David Munger. I think he wouldn't believe Michael when Michael denied that he was spy,' I said. 'Is that what happened, Michael?'

This time Michael managed to speak. His voice sounded like he was having trouble keeping in pitch.

'Tim did follow me to the Lock. I admit that. I saw him when I got there, playing spy games behind me. He acted like a madman. I couldn't reason with him. He just wouldn't listen to reason.'

'What reason?' Ron asked. His voice was quiet, but it held a threat. Michael responded by straightening up into his lecturer's pose.

'I had to meet David secretly,' he explained. 'There was too much at stake. He was involved in informing me on all aspects of South African security. We wouldn't, couldn't, take the risk that somebody would find out about it. That's why I never told a full meeting of this group. Bugging is too sophisticated and you never know, in these situations, who you can … '

'Trust,' Ron said. 'You couldn't trust us.'

Michael shrugged. He didn't look concerned. I thought he was misjudging Ron's mood. I thought he was making a mistake.

'Trust,' I said, 'is important, isn't it, Ron? That's why you kept information back from me. You wanted to protect your colleagues. Do you think you can go on doing that?'

Ron acted like he was at a tennis match. He looked at each of us in turn, as if waiting for some signal, and then he did it again. The seconds stretched until Aldwyn could stand it no longer.

'I must protest,' he said. 'Kate is treating us as if we are all guilty of something. Do not allow that to prejudice your actions, Ron.'

Ron might have been about to talk again, but Aldwyn's voice pulled him back. He put his hands and left it there, buried. I wanted to scream. I wanted to shake him out of his confusion. I wanted to leave. Instead, I took another breath and tried again. My last try.

'Let's go into details,' I said. 'Where did you go, Michael? After you picked up the papers on the Friday that Tim died?'

'What business is it of yours?' he said. He'd lost the battle for tone and his sentence almost ended in a shriek.

'Where did you go?' Ron said.

'I went … I went home … I think.' Michael said. 'How am I expected to remember?'

'What time did you reach home?' I asked.

'I don't remember,' he muttered.

'Who saw you? Where are the papers you picked up? What did

144

you do when you got home? You must remember. It's not so long ago and you have a good reason to remember.'

'What business is it of yours?' Michael repeated.

I felt like I'd reached the end of the line. That wasn't the only thing I felt. I felt relief: relief that I couldn't get any further, combined with the thought that maybe it didn't really matter. But I also felt like I'd screwed up. Reached the finale without properly doing my research, without checking out what Michael had done that day, where he had gone afterwards. It was as though I was ensuring that I couldn't finish the job — as if I was hoping I'd fail while appearing to try hard.

I was still trying to sort it out in my mind, when Ron spoke. He had removed his glasses and was looking straight at me, but his eyes were unfocused. He was a man responding to his own inner voice: a voice he, too, had been struggling with.

'I can't keep it to myself any longer,' he said. 'I no longer think I should. I've tried but it doesn't work. It's no good any longer.'

He turned his head. And this time his eyes were in focus when he looked at Michael. 'You knew about Tim's death before I told you, didn't you, Michael? I was the one who did the phoning round, but you knew before. Didn't you?'

Michael stuttered. 'David told me,' he said. 'He heard it over the wire at work.'

'INL isn't that kind of organisation,' I said. 'They're just a front. You killed Tim, didn't you?'

Michael nodded. And nodded again. And again. Ron and Aldwyn looked away.

'It was an accident,' Michael said. 'Just an accident. The lift doors were half-open ... or I opened them. I don't remember. I pushed him and he fell. It was horrible. I couldn't think what to do ... so I left. Walked away, hoping he was still alive, but knowing he wasn't. He provoked me, I swear it.'

'Was it about David?' I asked.

'I heard him arguing with that woman. Tim said all sorts of things. I couldn't believe him. When the woman left, I asked him for proof. He laughed at me. Said he'd got it all. Said Tina Schoenberg had told him some things about David that all fitted in. Tim said David had been arrested in South Africa and that he broke during the interrogation. Tim said David blamed his experience on the liberation movement and somewhere he wanted revenge. And then when Tim was … when I …'

'Finish now,' I said. I was surprised that my voice came out almost gently.

'David did believe the South Africans had killed Tim. That's why he tried to warn you off. He thought you would be in danger so he …'

'Yeah, I know … destroyed my saxophone.'

'I couldn't tell him about it then. I'm sorry Kate. I'm sorry … just sorry. Tim laughed at me. He said that he'd warned me and now he was going to expose David. My reputation would have been finished. I felt so angry … I pushed Tim. I didn't mean to kill him. I swear it. I didn't know what I was doing.'

His narration had tired him to his depths. He hung his head low and his shoulders shook.

'What are you going to do about it, Kate?' Ron asked.

'Not me,' I said. 'You. What are you going to do about it?'

15.

I went home and to sleep. I was back in Dalston.

It took about four days before I surfaced. In between my bouts of unconsciousness, I received a few phone calls. Joseph filled me in on the moves of the Home Office. They were investigating as slowly as possible. Anti-Apartheid made protests about South African police action in Britain, and the *Guardian* took them seriously for a couple of days. The Butcher no longer walked into South Africa House. INL closed down overnight. Red-faced Tories made loud denials that nobody believed and waited for the fuss to die down.

On the fifth day the phone rang twice. Ron called me. We didn't talk for long. He told me that Michael had gone away. Nobody knew when or whether he would return.

The phone call to Diana Nicholson lasted longer. She said that she wasn't going to keep Tim's unsigned will. She asked me if I would be a trustee. I agreed. She sounded sad, but she sounded like she'd come out the other end.

It took a month to solve the wrangles about money. I kept my temper while Aldwyn told me that the other groups were no longer prepared to fulfil their commitments. I kept it while he told me that, with Michael absent, nobody could release the money from AER. Eventually, the cheque came through the post.

Two months later I was standing in my room. It was a mess. When the phone rang I ran towards it, tripping on the case of my new alto. I fell and landed on Matthew's teddy bear. I picked it up and reached for the phone.

'Hell, Kate, I've got a proposal.'

'Aldwyn, hi. Long time, no see. Actually, I'm very busy at the moment. I've just found Matthew's long-lost teddy bear and even though I wouldn't steal from a five-year-old, finders keepers, don't you think?'

'Yes, Kate. Now could you listen? I have a proposal,' he said.

'Save it. The answer is no. No more detection … at least for a while.'

'It's not detection,' he said. 'The proposal is as follows: we are in the process of reorganising and we would like you to come and work with us. Ron and I both feel that an all-men collective can no longer function in this day and age. Come and work with us: name your conditions.'

I took a deep breath and held it in my chest. Then I slowly exhaled. It felt good.

'Not for me, Aldwyn,' I said. 'I'm otherwise engaged. In the middle of a vital task.'

I put the phone down on his protest. I turned back to my room with satisfaction. And then I cleaned it, until it sparkled.

Manuel Vazquez Montalban
Murder in the Central Committee

The Lights go out during a meeting of the Central Committee of the
Spanish Communist Party and Fernando Garrido, the general
secretary, is murdered. Pepe Carvalho is hired to find Garrido's
killer. His investigation shows that for both Stalinist hardliners and
Eurocommunists there is more than enough motive for the crime.

Pepe Carvalho, cynical bon viveur and inspired cook, is a detective
with a difference.

Murder in the Central Committee, already an international bestseller,
is the fourth book to feature Pepe Carvalho. Previous titles have won
both the (1979) Planeta Prize (the Spanish Booker) and the (1981)
Grand Prix of literary fiction in France.

Manuel Vazquez Montalban was born in 1939 in Barcelona, where
he still lives. He is a leading member of the Catalan Communist
Party and a professional writer, of novels, essays, reflections on
gastronomy and now detective novels.

0 86104 747 8   paperback   £3.50
0 86104 771 0   hardback   £7.95

Gordon Demarco
October Heat

Is Lana Birdwell being followed? Is she what she seems, a nice woman in trouble? She's just another client for Riley Kovachs, the shrewdest private eye since Marlowe. But the mob and big business are trying to stop socialist Upton Sinclair running for state governor and they bring a deadly edge to what seemed to be routine.

'*October Heat* moves as fast as a speeding bullet. It is without rival the first left-wing detective story. Dashiel Hammett himself would stand up and uncover for DeMarco's Riley Kovachs.'
San Francisco Chronicle.

Gordon DeMarco, ex-dishwasher, ex-chauffeur, ex-docker, is now a full-time writer in San Francisco. His other books include *Polish September* and *The Canvas Prison*, which stars Riley Kovachs and rebel actress Frances Farmer.

0 86104 744 3   paperback   £2.95
0 86104 770 2   hardback   £7.95

Nancy Milton
The China Option

In this pacey tale of menace, China is in turmoil. American bombs
and money are being used to support a hard-pressed government in a
US ploy against the Russians.

Anne Campbell, an American journalist in Peking, finds her articles
mysteriously spiked as she uncovers the story of a left-wing and
powerful opposition. Her lover is a diplomat, her passion is for
truth. But political intrigue defeats her in both.

'bureaucratic intrigue, historical speculation and frustrated love... the
first American thriller to deal satisfactorily with modern China.'
Washington Post

'Through (Nancy Milton's) eyes. We see a China we are rarely
privileged to see, and we are treated besides, to an all too plausible
scenario made immediate by first-hand knowledge and a crisp, no-
nonsense style.' *New York Times Book Review*

'An acute and sympathetic observer, Milton has every detail right.
From the garlicky smells of Peking's courtyards to the gauzy chiffon
scarves women wind around their drab Mao tunics in a bleak nod to
femininity.' *Los Angeles Times*

0 86104 746 X   paperback   £3.50
0 86104 772 9   hardback   £8.95

Ariel Dorfman
Widows

A political novel set ostensibly in Nazi-occupied Greece, but which could as well be Chile, Argentina, El Salvador or anywhere else today where people are 'disappeared'. Already a best seller in America, where it has been acclaimed as a 'masterpiece'.

'His beautifully understated tale is as powerful as it is moving'
Publishers Weekly

'Like any good Greek drama, this story is told about real characters who live and breathe, but somehow the meanings that mount and accrue around the action magnify everything beyond human proportions and the reader is constantly aware of being in the presence of universal truths.' Barbara Raskin

0 86104 723 0   hardback   £7.95
paperback published by Abacus

Pluto books are available through your local bookshop. In case of difficulty contact Pluto to find out local stockists or to obtain catalogues/leaflets (Telephone 01-482 1973).
If all else fails write to:

> **Pluto Press Limited**
> **Freepost** (no stamp required)
> **The Works**
> **105A, Torriano Avenue**
> **London NW5 1YP**

To order, enclose a cheque/p.o. payable to Pluto Press to cover price of book, plus 50p per book for postage and packing (£2.50 maximum).